"Nina K. Hoffman's *Catalyst* is a marvel of inventiveness, beautifully realized in close sensory detail."
— KATE WILHELM, author of *Where Late the Sweet Birds Sang* and *Storyteller*

"Charming, inventive, and weird. Hoffman's aliens and their environment are fascinating. And the humans? As always, the author saves a dash of compassion even for the person with the most disagreeable personality."
— BRUCE HOLLAND ROGERS, author of *Thirteen Ways to Water and Other Stories*

"Nobody does down the rabbit (or spider) hole like Nina Kiriki Hoffman. Sometimes when you read, you get a peek into an entirely different mind. This is one of those reads. Everything is so strange in this book but also strangely true. Not what you expect, no matter what you expect."
— RAY VUKCEVICH, author of *Meet Me in the Moon Room*

"Nina Hoffman is one of my favorite writers, period. I never know what I'm getting into when I open a book of hers, but I always know it will be smart, maybe funny, with characters I can care about, and beautifully written. When they were handing out talent, I think she got way more than her fair share—but I'm happy for that."
— CHARLES DE LINT, author of *Widdershins* and *The Blue Girl*

CATALYST

Catalyst

NINA KIRIKI HOFFMAN

TACHYON PUBLICATIONS | SAN FRANCISCO

Cover design: Ann Monn
Interior design & typography: John D. Berry
The typeface is Mercury.

Tachyon Publications
1459 18th Street #139
San Francisco, CA 94107
(415) 285-5615
www.tachyonpublications.com

Series Editor: Jacob Weisman

ISBN 10: 1-892391-38-4
ISBN 13: 978-1-892391-38-4

Printed in the United States of America
by the Maple-Vail Manufacturing Group

First Edition: 2006

9 8 7 6 5 4 3 2 1

OCT 2 6 2006

To Eileen Gunn, who discovered me.

CATALYST

1

KASLIN STUMBLED ON the alien city by accident three months after he and his parents arrived on Chuudoku. He was running from Histly, a girl in his midteen edsection whose parents had had her augmented, and whose augmentations included self-defense mechanisms she used to hurt people who weren't even attacking her. She'd assaulted him with three different fingertip poisons already. One of them put him to sleep. Another made him puke repeatedly, and left his stomach so sore he couldn't sit up for a day. The third paralyzed him, so he was wide awake but unable to move away when she leaned down over him and pressed her lips on his. He had managed to moan, but he couldn't stop her kissing him. She mashed his lips against his teeth, and he couldn't move away.

Only half his class had been watching, but of course they told the rest, and people in other sections, too. Later they made moaning noises at him wherever he went.

The first time Kaslin saw Histly, across the quad the day he started school, he had liked her looks. She had shaggy pink hair, long on top and down the back of her head, short on the sides, and she had a wrestler's build, muscular and taut. She was a head taller than he was. She stood with an easy arrogance, like every woman character he'd ever fantasized about in simgames, where he'd spent most of his time since his dad's disgrace. Simgames had kept him tranced during his family's stretch in the refugee camp on Hitherto before they shipped out, and all the time in steerage on the ship to Chuudoku.

She looked like his ideal woman, but he never imagined she'd notice him. He was just another skinny, sun-starved immigrant kid; boatloads of them arrived on Chuudoku every day, though most of those were part of the penal populations destined for drug trials, and didn't end up in the public schools. Kaslin figured he could study Histly enough to get her into his dreams without her even seeing him, but he was wrong. The first time he stared at her for more than a minute, she turned and stared back. They were both in class, waiting for the chemistry sim to start on their interactive desk terminals. Kaslin didn't drop his eyes: Histly's were such a strange crystalline green he couldn't look away. "Don't face her, don't face her, drop your gaze," muttered the lanky boy in the next seat, but Kaslin hadn't been able to focus on anything but Histly.

Kaslin saw Histly and thought, yum. Histly saw Kaslin and thought, prey. After that first day, Kaslin saw Histly and thought, run.

Whenever she saw him, Histly chased him. He ran, she chased; if she caught him, she did something awful. Her leg muscles were augmented, too, so she could catch him in a flat-out race. He had to be cunning to get away.

He ran a different direction every time. This time, he wove through a spike tree grove. He was smaller and thinner than Histly. Maybe he could squeeze between trees where she couldn't fit. Could she break through the spikes? He'd seen a report about spike trees—part of his basic introductory training for living on Chuudoku—which said the spikes had a Mohs hardness of eight. Were Histly's augmentations stronger than that?

He'd never been in this particular spike tree grove before. He heard Histly following, her big augmented feet crushing the brittle, white, diamond-leafed underbrush.

Even though they were both running, Histly had plenty of breath to yell, "Oh, Kas, you are going to flitch a clister when I catch you. You are going to plutch. Just you wait and see what I've got for you now. I have five more fingertips to try on you, and my thumbs can do things, too. Just you wait."

He didn't want to wait. He eeled between trees and slipped on a smooth, dark, glassy piece of ground. Before he could stop himself, he screamed. *Wump!* Contact with the ground forced the air out of his lungs, and he couldn't get it back.

Histly's big feet crunched closer, and she laughed her evil laugh. Could her other poisons be worse than the ones she'd used on him already? He needed to hack into the med center database and find out exactly what to be afraid of. Maybe he was better off not knowing.

He managed to gulp air again, only it oomphed out of him in wheezes, and he knew those would give him away, too. He pushed painfully to his knees, his head throbbing where he'd hit it on a spike tree trunk on his way down. His vision was blurry. He saw a dark gap in the ground, half-hidden by spike leaves not too far away, and crawled in that direction. The ground didn't hurt him now that he was in such intimate touch with it. He crawled over a carpet of shed spikes. Once the trees let go of the spikes, they turned soft; Kaslin had had a couple of fights with his friend and partment neighbor Maya using soft spikes, back when she was still speaking to him, before the moaning and kiss noises started whenever he walked through a room.

Histly was the reason he was so alone. She was about to poison him yet again, but once he recovered, if he ever did, he should take the fight to her. He could think up a lot of scary things to do to her, even without augmentation.

He was approaching the dark thing. It was kind of a cave. Maybe there would be some Chuudoku animal in it that he'd never heard of. Maybe something that ate people. No, there was nothing here that ate people, though some of the animals with sharp teeth might nibble until they realized they couldn't digest humans. A lot of them had poisons or narcotics in their spit. They could irritate and immobilize you, but most of them couldn't kill you. Those were small animals, no bigger than midsize dogs; you could kick them away before they really bit if you had good shoes.

Maybe the cavedweller was something that farted on people, and it would leave a stink on him.

Anything was better than Histly.

He crawled into the cave. The floor was dirt to start with, but changed to a soft surface, pale, waxy, and layered. It smelled like wall polish and burnt sugar. He had trouble getting traction on it. What if it was the secretions of something monstrous? Some kind of solid spider web?

Still had to be better than Histly.

He kept going, skating on hands and knees over the sugary, slithery surface. Flakes of it came loose, powdered his dark green cargo pants, caught in the folds of his yellow shirt. Even loose, the stuff was more slippery than slow.

The cave dipped, and he slid down into total darkness, a slide that felt like it went on for half an hour. He kept gaining speed, and wondered what he'd hit when he came to the bottom, if he ever did. Air rushed past his face. It felt like the cave was swallowing him.

The angle of his slide changed until he was scooting across a flat floor. Though there was very little drag in the slippery surface, he felt himself slowing. He slid into a deep drift of something soft and powdery. It stopped him, but didn't rise up to choke him. It smelled like oil and oranges.

After he brushed powder off his face and chest, caught his breath, and gave his heart time to slow down, he struggled to his feet. He lost his footing and slid farther. He couldn't see anything, but he liked the feel of walking across this strange, slippery surface. It was a little like snow, without the cold and the cutting edges of ice. Falling didn't hurt. He wished he knew how to skate. He got up again and tried to glide forward, arms outstretched. Where were the walls?

Again he fell, this time on his stomach. He slid through a clump of powder and plunged down another slope in the darkness, his clothes waxy with the substance he was sliding across, his breathing unimpaired. His mouth tasted like butter and garlic.

Finally the slope flattened. He slid to a stop.

He rolled over, lay on his back, and stared up into darkness. Somewhere up there hung a faint radiance, a dim pink glow. It looked very far away. He wondered what it was. Maybe his eyes would adjust and he'd be able to see his surroundings. He felt comfortable. The air was cool but not cold. The ground was soft under him, clotted and slick with powdery, waxy debris, but still fragrant: oil, oranges, burnt sugar. He patted it with his hands. Something soapy that gave way to pressure. Shapes stuck up from the ground, but when he clutched them, they crumbled before he could tell what they were.

He thought: I'm happy. No way is Histly going to follow me down here.

"Bootah," said something. "Bink," said a whisper from another direction. "Blook," said a third.

Kaslin was terrified. Who was in here with him? What language were they speaking? Chuudoku was a Class G colony, a human settlement on a planet registered as devoid of sentient life, though there was evidence that once an alien civilization had existed here. There was even a little museum in the town hall that housed a few small, boring artifacts. Kaslin had written a report on them for school in Ash. The eighteen items on display were all white, rounded things that didn't look like tools or weapons. None of them had any pictures carved or painted on them. They were just things that apparently didn't occur in nature. Chemical and electronic tests on the items indicated they had once been touched and shaped; but there was no apparent cultural content. He had written a pretty short report.

"Bink," whispered a voice from above him. The pink spot on the ceiling brightened a fraction.

"Who are you? What do you want?" he yelled, much louder than he meant to. His voice traveled away from him, fading with distance. He got a sense of the size of the cavern. It felt enormous. He struggled to sit up, but every time he placed his hands and pushed, they slid away. He wriggled around until he was lying on his stomach, and then he carefully inched his way upward using knees and hands at the same time. He managed to get all the way to his feet before he slipped and fell on his face again.

"Bink bink bink," whispered something near him. Light bloomed on the wall.

Oh, well. If whatever was talking to him wanted to come eat him, there wasn't anything he could do about it.

"Bootah," said something else to his left.

He turned toward it. "Bootah," he said.

"Blook." This was a higher voice, to his right.

He turned again. "Blook."

"Bootah bootah bootah." Something above him, as far away as the pinkly glowing ceiling of the cavern.

"Bootah bootah bootah," Kaslin echoed, feeling reckless. If this was something's idea of communication, he was all for it. He only wished he knew what they were talking about.

"Blook." Just beside him.

"Blook," he repeated.

Something happened to the surface he lay on. Its waxy, soapy feel turned a little gritty. He tried again to rise, found this time that there was enough traction for him to manage. "Blook. Blook blook blook," he muttered. He took a couple of steps. The ground was solid...for eight paces, anyway, before he slipped.

He put his hand palm down on the slippery surface, slid it back and forth to feel the wax there. "Blook. Blook blook." Under his palm, the surface morphed, gritted, solidified.

Wow.

There were all kinds of voice-activated machines and commands in the smart partment he lived in with his parents. You could shift views in the windowwalls with a word, change the colors of your furniture, turn things on and off; but he hadn't encountered this kind of textural change before.

What had the voices been saying when he was lying on his back? "Bink," he said. "Bink."

The radiance from the ceiling brightened. Each syllable he said made a different spot glow, most of the glows pink or yellow.

"Bink. Bink bink bink bink—" He had to stop. It was almost too bright in here to see. He didn't know a word to make things go dark again. Lack of forethought.

He repeated words to make the floor harden, and walked forward. Now that he could see, he realized that the cavern's roof varied in height, that stalactites and stalagmites toothed the edges of the cavern. Some of the pink glows from his chorus of binks shone reflected from sheeted water that lay in the lowest floors.

It took him a while to notice how beautiful this underground place was.

If there was only something to eat here, he could stay here forever. Well, okay, water that he knew was safe to drink would be nice, too, and maybe something to read. No weather to worry about; the air was cool but not cold, and there was all this white stuff. "Blook blook blook," he said, and dashed forward, then skidded through soapy surface he hadn't spoken into solid yet. He laughed as his feet slid out from under him. Even full-length on the slippery floor, he kept sliding until he crashed into a stalagmite. The collision wasn't hard enough to hurt. He sat up laughing and scrubbed soft flakes out of his hair.

Then he heard something chilling.

"Kas! Kas! You slimy scutchbag, where are you? I heard you laughing!"

Oh, shrike, Histly!

"Bsstu," whispered something nearby. The pink glow in the ceiling, walls, and floor dimmed a fraction.

"Bsstu bsstu bsstu!" he cried. With each syllable, the light faded. "Bsstu bsstu bsstu," whispered Kaslin, calling down utter dark.

"Hey!" yelled Histly. And then a neon-blue light shone some distance off, a handheld that sprayed blue light over Histly's front and her grinning face. "Not so fast." She held up the light toward him, and Kaslin realized he was sitting right out in the open where she could see him. She strode toward him over the path he had paved earlier with blooks.

"Buk buk buk," something prompted him from the left.

"Buk buk buk," he whispered, and felt the flakes beneath him soften into powder. "Buk buk buk." The white soapy powder swallowed him, closed over his head.

"Hey!" screamed Histly. "Hey! What? Wait!" Then she was coughing and struggling in her own wasteland of soapy flakes. She screamed, a scream that smothered into a gargling yelp.

Kaslin swam away, waved his arms, kicked his feet, somehow propelled himself. He hoped he was heading away from Histly. He couldn't hear her anymore, but he wasn't sure whether it was because he was far from her or she had stopped struggling. Had the ground smothered her? Would it smother him?

He tried to breathe, and the flakes clogged his nose and mouth, broke in a burnt sugar taste on his tongue. Then they melted, and the tastes shifted in his mouth and nose. He tasted flowermilk and spun sugar, apricot. He swallowed, and more flakes came into his mouth, with another constellation of tastes, different fruits, some he had never tasted before, sweet, juicy with his saliva. He swallowed and the growls of his stomach quieted.

He turned his head away from the direction he swam and found that he could breathe without pulling flakes into his mouth. He was ready to explore more of their taste, and damn the consequences—alien, untested, maybe indigestible, maybe poison, or mutagenic—but not while he was engaged in trying to escape. He swam below the surface of the flakes, and waited for whispers to lead him somewhere. He hadn't been able to swim in water for two years now. He had loved the ocean when he was younger, but his father had lost rights to Hitherto citizenship for Kaslin, Kaslin's mother, and himself. Father was machine smart and scheme stupid. He could never resist anything that looked like it might lead to easy money, and he never learned how to cover his tracks. The family had been locked up in a refugee camp for almost two years before headhunters from Chuudoku recruited his father, who had particular talents with machines. Chuudoku was not a pleasant planet. Most large bodies of water here were too full of mineral salts, nasty, biting pseudofish, and possible toxins to swim in.

"Blook," Kaslin muttered sometime later, when he had swum what felt like a long way. "Blook blook blook blook." Beneath him, the surface hardened, but above and around him it hardened, too; he encased himself in a rock cocoon. "Buk buk buk," he whispered, and again he was in a lake of aerated flakes. He swam up until he broke the surface into airy darkness. He listened and looked. No light at all, and no sounds from Histly.

"Bink," said Kaslin. A glow bloomed in a nearby stalagmite,

showed him a section of cave that looked different from where he had been before. He struggled up out of the flakes, whispered blooks until he was lying on his own island. He crawled to the edge, dipped his hand into still-soft flakes, lifted them, and took a bite. They had a waxy texture, but then they melted and he tasted melon and cassua fruit and something else less sweet but juicy, a cucumber taste without the seeds. He picked up handfuls of flakes and said, "Blook blook blook," to them. They hardened into jagged rocks in his hands.

What about—he shaped snowshoes for himself, spoke softly enough to them that the shoes hardened without attaching to hardened ground. He spoke straps that melded to the shoes, fixing them on his feet. He rolled out poles for himself, spoke them hard. Wow, this stuff—it was great. He skated through the cavern, speaking light as he went. This place was his. The voices had given it to him. Histly couldn't scare him anymore now that he had his own powers. He followed his own trail of stirred-up flakes—his passing beneath the surface had left a lasting wake—and headed back to the first cavern, speaking faint light as he went.

With her augmented legs, Histly had cleared a pit for herself. All her struggles had only gotten her deeper into the white stuff, about three meters down. Kaslin heard her cursing before he saw what she had done. He softened his shoes enough to take them off, then whispered a path for himself up to the edge of the pit. He crouched there and stared down at her.

The cold blue light flashed up into his face. He squinted against it.

"Don't just stand there!" she screamed. "Help me out of here!"

"How?"

"How come it's solid where you are?" she yelled. "How did you get out once you sank under the surface?"

"I swam out."

She screamed and ran toward the wall he perched on. He had only hardened a little crust of the very top. He pushed back, sliding along his path as she crashed through the softer flakes below it, stirring up waves without rising toward the surface.

How *had* he risen? Muttered enough hardness to the flakes to give him purchase, then swam up. He had muttered, the way he was muttering now. He thought what he wanted the flakes to do and muttered the right word. The environment had taught him how to shape it.

"Kaslin! You sneaky, slimy scutbucket, you go get some help and get me out of here!" Histly yelled after she had flurried through flakes and dug herself an extension of the pit. The beam of her blue light scythed up out of the hole, flashed across roof teeth, blinded Kaslin momentarily, moved on. Histly crouched on the bottom of her pit and sprang upward, striving for the lip. But even when she got the height, she crashed into more collapsible, compactable flakes and flurried down into the pit again in a cloud of disturbed neon-blue scatter, her light spinning as it left her hand and casting odd shadows.

"Okay," Kaslin said. "I'm going now." He reformed his snowshoe straps, muttered an occasional blook to harden the floor just enough for walking, and poled off into darkness, poking ahead of him with the poles to feel for stalagmites. He wasn't going to share his light with her.

"Bring food and water when you come back!" she screamed, the sound echoing from the ceiling and distant hollows.

"Bink," said Kaslin once he figured he was far enough away. She wouldn't turn off her light, so if he used just a little, she might not notice. Again he was in a portion of the cave that didn't look familiar. It occurred to him that he didn't even know which way the exit was. Plus, he had come down two slopes: how was he going to climb back up?

He could form pitons from floor stuff, he supposed.

Go for help.

Why?

Everything that made his life on Chuudoku hell was in a pit in the soap flakes behind him. All he had to do was forget about her. Eventually, he would figure out how to get out of here; he didn't have to tell anybody Histly was here. He didn't have to tell anybody about this cavern at all. It could be his refuge and retreat while he learned more about this alien stuff.

Histly could just...disappear.

"Bink," Kaslin muttered. "Bink bink bink." The air around him felt different, less free. As he binked light into being, he saw why: the walls had narrowed and were channeling him into a tunnel. He wondered if it would lead him back to the surface. He would have to make some decisions once he got out.

This way didn't look familiar at all. Then again, he hadn't really seen the place where he came in; he had been sliding too fast, and it had been dark.

"Bink," he said. The voices in the ceiling echoed him. They were closer now, and sounded more like other people. Pink light bloomed in splotches on the walls around him. He glanced here and there. Dark shadows loomed in the walls by some of the lightspots. He walked toward one and found a face.

An alien. His whole life he'd dreamed of making first contact with a new species. It was the future he'd choose if he ever had enough credit to buy an upper-level career module. At first that had seemed impossible. But just before they left Hitherto, his mother had bought a med-tech career module with carefully hoarded savings from their food allowance and money she'd annexed when Kaslin's father had won bets and come home to their tent in the refugee camp drunk. The career module took. Since she arrived on Chuudoku, she'd gotten a good job with the gov, her credit going to an account Kaslin's father couldn't access. She was saving for Kaslin's future. Kaslin started dreaming again.

Discovery of an alien tomb. Maybe he could parlay that into a down payment on his future.

He placed his hand against the wall over the face, a nearly transparent surface, like clear ice. The texture was smooth, not cold. The face was not human. It had a flat, oval, brown surface wider than his head, with three domed oblongs in a triangular formation on the top half, edged at their lower ends with a thin flutter of black lace; they looked like giant closed eyes. Below them, a slit ran lengthwise almost across the face, curved up at either end like the mouth of a turtle. The face had five small appendages along its upper edge, stalks with round, flower-faced, funnel-shaped openings on them, aimed toward the tunnel and Kaslin.

"Bink," he whispered, and the light grew, glistened off the clear surface over the face.

"Buk," he said. His thumb plunged through the glassy window, stubbed against something harder below. "Buk buk buk." Gently he brushed clear flakes away from the face, until he touched its brown/bronze skin, expecting ice cold and stillness.

But the skin was smooth, elastic, and warm. A muscle under it moved.

He screamed and jerked back, tumbled in a welter of pale soapy flakes to the floor of the tunnel. He dug down into the flakes, scuffing them up until he had cleared a hole big enough to hide in. He dropped into it and pulled flakes from the piles at the sides until he was up to his shoulders in soft, soapy feathers. His breath hissed in and out. He glanced up at the face.

Its eyes were open. All three of them, dark, glistening, fixed on him. Its lipless mouth seemed to be smiling.

"Bsstu," Kaslin muttered. Darkness would make it go away. Or maybe not. Darkness would make it grow. He didn't dim the light any further.

"Bootah," whispered the face.

"Bootah," Kaslin said. He glanced around, trying to see what "bootah" accomplished, but he didn't notice anything different about the illumination or the consistency of the flakes.

"Bootah bist bist bit," it said; he saw its mouth move, splitting and shaping, a dark cavern behind it, something shadowy moving within. The small fleshy flowers around its forehead swiveled on their stalks, aiming this way and that. Then the wall erupted.

Kaslin squawked. A flurry of "buk's" ran out of his mouth and he dug down into the softening soap, longing only for complete encasement. What had he just seen? Six, eight, ten dark drills plunging out around the face he had uncovered, drills that broke through into air and spread fans of flat petal-shaped fingers that brushed each other off.

What had he awakened in the wall?

He licked flakes from his lips, chewed several mouthfuls of cinnamon-grape-melon. He cleared out a little pocket near his face. "Blook," he said, over and over, until the ground closed around him like concrete.

Silence.

"Bink," he whispered, and a faint flower of pink light blossomed above his face. He was caught in a prison he had made for himself. He felt safe.

The earth shook and shifted. His inner ears answered; his sense of balance told him he was tilting, cocoon and all, lifting, sliding, moving somewhere fast. "Bootah," he muttered, the taste of jelly on his tongue. He didn't know what "bootah" did. He felt dizzy. Time passed while his senses told him he was tilting, traveling, bouncing in the grip of something he couldn't see.

Finally the momentum stopped. He waited, encased in his self-made coffin, wondering what next.

2

Sound came through his walls: "Buk buk buk buk," in several voices. With each word the concrete encasing him softened. Why had he thought he could protect himself against the people who had taught him how to control the white stuff? "Bink," said one voice, several times, and, "Bamba bamba bamba," said another. Something stirred the flakes away from him, uncovering him with gentle brushings and swipes. He closed his eyes, felt furry, bristled things sweep over him, dusting off the flakes. Finally he looked up, into five of the three-eyed faces, with their swiveling, fleshy flowers. Their eyes had no whites, just darks that shone as though wet. "Bist," said one. It lifted a hand—eight flat, bristle-covered fingers rayed around a circular palm—and brushed a few final flakes from his cheeks. Another hand combed through his hair. A third fingered his clothes.

The creatures had short, squat, three-part bodies: heads, thoraxes, abdomens. Their heads were positioned forward atop their thoraxes, and their many long, multi-jointed limbs came from the central section, like spiders' legs, only more numerous. Below the leg nests were round, backward-bent bulbs of brown, bristle-covered abdomens with folds and pockets in them. Fur or clothing?

One face leaned forward, thrust itself against his hair. The mouth opened—he felt its damp, hot breath against his scalp, smelled a sudden flood of flower—and then it nipped. A tug on his scalp, a clipping sound. The face lifted away, chewing, a rustle rather than a crunch. He raised a hand to his head. No blood wet his palm; he hadn't felt a bite.

The first face spoke to a second one, and that leaned down, too, and bit near his other ear. The same tug. When this one lifted away, he saw a few short ends of his hair sticking out of its closed mouth. It chewed, nodded sideways at the first face. It spoke a rapid stream of syllables, and then there were four more nipping at his hair. He closed his eyes again and waited for teeth to break his skin. Instead, a succession of sharp tugs, chewing, murmurs, and finally wet, raspy pressure against his scalp from several directions. A huff of flower breath against his face, and the touch of a tongue skating over his cheek, licking up his tears. A murmur. Another tongue on his other cheek, a gentle prodding with its tip against his closed eyelid, seeking the source of the salt water, perhaps. He wished he could stop crying. His only comfort came in the thought that they didn't know what it meant.

Was his hair the appetizer before the main course?

Then they turned him over, their hands tugging on his clothes, sliding inside the neckhole of his shirt and up under the hem, bristly fingers slipping up his sleeves and the cuffs of his pants. They stripped off his toolbelt. One of them discovered the stiktites that fastened his shirt and pants shut, figured out the pressure that released them. They played with the internal thong of his pants, unfastened the stiktites there, too, brushed against his penis. He tried to reach down to cover himself. Strange hands circled his wrists and forearms, pulled them out straight—nothing rough, gentle but implacable tugs.

They stripped him, many hands touching him from all directions. The bristles on their fingers were soft but scraping. They licked all the hair off his body, long, gentle strokes. He couldn't help his arousal at so many soft, intimate touches, just the right sort of raspy roughness. They were interested in that change at his groin, interested with hands and tongues—pressure, but no injury; squeezing without squishing. Their tongues were as big as hands, and could change shape the way human tongues could, be broad or narrow, long or short, but always flexible, muscular, and slightly rough. Soon enough he was jerking in their hold, his groin pumping as they stroked him, something he couldn't stop. Was this the best thing that had ever happened to him, or the worst? It felt like heaven.

They licked up his ejaculate, caressed him as he wilted, cupped and fondled every part of him.

God! What kind of first contact was this? What if he'd screwed up relations with an alien race forever? Why couldn't he control himself? He tried to curl up into a ball, cover his face with his hands, tuck his feet up against his underside, but they kept exploring, not licking him anymore, tugging on his limbs, stretching them out to full extension, bending them at the joints gently this way and that—never so far that he hurt; exploring the way he worked, he guessed. One furry finger tugged at his lower lip until he opened his mouth, then dipped inside to feel his teeth, brushed over his tongue. It tasted syrup sweet and dusty, the bristles soft. He sucked on it, and it stopped moving, the other fingers of its hand cupping his chin. Presently it slid out of his mouth, and one of the others sifted some waxy flakes into his mouth, these like warm but still-solid ice cream, smooth and sweet with an intensity of fruit flavor. He sucked and swallowed, sucked and swallowed as they fed him more. Furred fingers rested on his throat as he swallowed, not impeding him, rippling as his esophagus rippled. Others stroked his belly. Others kept up a steady flow of touch and exploration, going over the same ground again. He was almost too embarrassed to look at them, but he looked: he was surrounded. Maybe the reason they kept touching him was because more and more of them arrived, and each of them wanted contact.

It all happened in shuffling silence.

He felt so tired he forgot to worry about when they were going to eat him. One of them slid something into his mouth that tasted like cherries. He fell asleep, cocooned in alien touches.

When he woke, later, he had no idea how much time had passed. The aliens still held him stretched out, but there were fewer of them surrounding him. He felt strange. Not sick. Not hungry, either. Different, as though he'd lost his balance and he was shifting around inside. He swallowed several times. His mouth tasted of mint.

Someone set him on his feet. Someone handed him his clothes. Confused and shaky, he dressed himself in the midst of a forest of brown limbs and spider bodies bigger than his own body. His skin was so smooth now. He ran his hand over his head: bare. Even his eyebrows were gone. He remembered those nibbling kisses; they didn't exactly have teeth inside their mouths, just some sort of cutting plates on top and bottom that together acted like delicate scissors, strangely erotic, hard to think about. He couldn't tell whether he should be grossed out or flattered. For sure he must look strange now.

"Bootah," said someone. "Bamba bisti buell."

Kaslin swallowed. His mouth was dry. He felt like he was the stupidest person he knew. What had he been thinking, surfing around on soap, eating it randomly when it hadn't been tested, speaking words in a language he didn't know? Everything he had done since he fell in this hole violated rules of planetary exploration and alien contact. Forget the fact that Chuudoku had been certified a Class G planet, no known sentience, and that the colony had already been here for more than two hundred T-standard years (one hundred sixty-three Chuudoku years) and that there were no records of giant spider aliens. He'd dreamed of being an explorer ever since he watched a skipvid about great planetary discoveries by the Explorer Corps when he was five. He and his parents had been living in a holding pen on Hitherto at the time, before his father had managed to come back from nothing and start over—Hitherto gave people second and third chances. His father had used them all up.

Kaslin had always wanted to go somewhere no other humans had been, meet aliens other people hadn't encountered yet. He'd been studying first contact manuals most of his life.

He'd so totally blown it with these guys.

Well, maybe not completely. He hadn't threatened them. They weren't at all scared of him.

Why should they be? All he'd done was run and hide. Great way to make a first impression.

Someone licked his head. The tongue was warm and only slightly damp; it felt nice. Another traced his ear with its tongue. He shivered, felt a rise in his lower self. Okay, so he'd done more than run and hide, but not on purpose. Would they know that?

Maybe the one who licked his head was just looking for more hair to eat. Maybe he was a hair factory to them, a walking popsicle tree.

If they kept it up, he'd embarrass himself again.

When one of them licked his neck, he flinched. "Please," he said, then had to cough to clear his throat. "Please stop."

"Bootah? Bootah bisti?"

"Bootah bisti," he said. *Never use a native word if you don't know what it means*, he remembered from one of the explorer's manuals he'd read. How was he supposed to figure out what words meant if he couldn't use them? He never would have binked and blooked and bukked his way this far without experimenting.

They stopped licking him. A hand cupped a pile of flakes near his face. One flat finger tapped at his chin. He opened his mouth, and the hand eased some of the flakes in. These tasted like fresh bread, and made his stomach happy. He opened his mouth again, and was fed.

Something thrashed in the distance, a ripple that moved through the forest of legs and brown bodies around him.

"Kaslin!" Histly screeched. He jerked at the lash of her voice. "Kaslin, I'll kill you! I swear! Next time I get my nails on you, you're a dead man!"

He lifted his hands, reached into the alien hand holding the food flakes at his mouth height, brushed the flakes into his own cupped hand. He chewed, sucked, and swallowed, then stuck the leftovers in his pocket before she arrived. He wanted to be ready to run.

Another furry hand offered him a pile of flakes, and he stuffed his pocket with them.

Histly didn't come under her own power. She was carried toward him: six of the aliens held her, each using at least three hands to immobilize her. They walked in concert with each other, arm/legs interweaving. Nobody muzzled Histly, but they didn't let her move her arms or legs.

"How could you do this to me?" she screamed. The aliens set her down three feet from him. He backed up, afraid they'd let her go and she'd make good on her threat to kill him. Flower hands steadied and stopped him. Histly's captors didn't let go of her. "Do you know what these things did to me? They stripped me! They probed me! They did something to my hands so I can't move my fingers! They unsizzled my legs so I can't kick. They *licked* me! All over and up inside!"

He studied her. She still had most of her head hair and all of her eyebrows. He touched the top of his head, felt its nakedness.

"You were supposed to go for help, you stupid clister!"

Her carriers brought her closer, angled her face toward his, until they were almost kissing close. Hands on his arms and shoulders held him steady. What were the aliens doing?

"You midit! You midge! You cracker of all good luck!" she screamed, and spat in his face. "I am really and truly going to kill you for this!" She struggled, her arm muscles bulging between furry brown fingers. Her hands hung limp from her wrists, though, so maybe she had spoken the truth: they had paralyzed her weapons.

Kaslin wiped spit from his face and pressed against the legs behind him. He turned and slipped between some of the legs, ducked under dangling abdomens. At first the aliens fenced him in, but then they stepped aside and let him go.

"Bouzula?" someone murmured. Most of them stroked him as he passed, but they didn't stop him. "Bai? Bilia?"

He reached the outer edge of the circle of aliens. They were gathered in a large cavern, with a high ceiling and pale walls spotted with glowing pink splotches. Several tunnels led away from here. He didn't know which would be best; he'd been encased in his cocoon when they brought him here, and he had no idea of direction.

He glanced back. Histly hung where he had left her, held up by alien arms, cursing and struggling without effect. "You better not leave me here," she screamed. "You'll regret it if you do!"

"Bink," he muttered, and fled down the nearest tunnel.

"Kaslin! Kaslin, don't go! Please don't go!" Her wail had an element of terror in it now. He remembered how scared he had been not that long ago, when he had been aroused and also terrified that they were going to dismember and eat him. He wasn't sure why he'd stopped being afraid. Maybe because they had let go of him.

"Bink bink bink." Constellations of pink glows lighted his way, more springing up on walls, ceiling, and floor ahead of him as he walked. He heard shuffling through the flake floor behind him. He stopped, and three of the aliens caught up with him. He looked up at the nearest one's face. It blinked all three eyes one after another, stroked a hand over his head, then gave a little push in the middle of his back. He stumbled, started walking again.

There was a chance he would never get out of here. At least there was plenty to eat. He angled toward a wall, bukked at it, rubbed off a few flakes of soapy substance and tasted them.

Vinegar over potatoes. He paused with the taste on his tongue, trying to decide whether he liked it. He put some in one of his pockets for later, keeping it separate from the bread flakes he'd stored before.

Of course, no telling if any of this was nutritious. There were programs for gene combining between Terran and Chuudoku plants; it was one of the high priority colony experiments, adapting people to the planet and the planet to people. He and his parents had had to undergo a battery of government gene-mods so they could survive comfortably on the planet.

Some of the plant experiments were successful. Chuudoku had four or five new kinds of fruit that had been developed here, and his mother bought lots of the pink kind, even though to Kaslin it left an aftertaste like burnt rubber. Nutritious and cheap, she said, and gave him cola to cut the taste. He guessed he'd find out if a diet of soap flakes actually fed him. If not, his stomach should complain sometime soon. He checked his wrist for the time—he was sure it had been hours since he'd eaten human food, and that should tell him something. The face of his implanted chrono was scraped. He tapped it to light it and saw only a bruised blur.

They had licked it. They had scratched the implant's surface with their tongues. Sheesh. If their tongues could scratch a sup-posedly unbreakable implant, what had they done to his skin? He rubbed his wrist. Still hairless, and the skin felt—strangely smooth.

"Bizouli," said one of the aliens.

"Bizouli?" he repeated, then glanced around to see if he could tell what that word did. Nothing visible. He wanted to make a dictionary.

A hand stroked from his forehead over his skull and down his neck, over his shoulder and along his arm. Another tapped his back, and he started forward. "So we're headed somewhere?" he said. "Is there something you want me to do?" They walked behind and beside him. He kept going.

Eventually the tunnel widened into another huge cavern. The flake floor here was softer than new snow; he skidded and plowed down into it by mistake, buried himself up to his shoulders. The aliens moved their feet quickly, in a strange dance that kept them skating along the top.

"Boo boo boo," one muttered as it paused beside him, its feet in constant motion.

"Boo boo boo!" The other two spoke at different pitches, and the syllables came out with different timing. Kaslin realized they were laughing at him. At least, he thought they were.

"Boo boo," he muttered. "Blook blook blook."

Flakes hardened enough that he could scramble up on top of the surface again. He pulled up flakes and shaped another pair of snowshoes. One of the aliens ran its hands over his creation. He waited, then strapped the shoes to his feet with strands of blooked flake. He struggled up. The aliens laughed and stroked and patted him.

As they crossed the cavern, he saw plowed-up ground, skid marks, holes in the floor. That stalagmite poking up through the flakes, with its mushroom top surmounted by a thick, snowy layer of flakes—he was sure he'd seen it before.

They crossed more floor and he found long sliding scrapes, with others overlapping them.

This was where he'd slid down from the upper world, with Histly behind him. Was he about to get out? He raced to the far slope, started up it, slid down. He tried to get a grip on some of the stone projections that stuck up through the snow of flakes. He pulled himself partway up the slope, but then he slipped on waxy flakes and slid down again, slipping under the surface of the flakes. He had to laugh.

He'd had a thought: make pitons, the same way he had made snowshoes. He shaped stakes of flakes and spoke blook to them, but before he could finish enough hardness to pick his way up, one of the aliens wrapped an arm around him and tugged him all the way to the top of the first slope, clinging to one protrusion after another. "Beck," it muttered. "Beck beck."

"Beck," said Kaslin. The floor got sticky. "Beck beck beck beck beck!"

He was stuck fast, and so was the alien who was helping him. The floor had turned to tar. "Boo," said the alien, tossing its head back. A little string of boos came from its mouth. The other two, who had stayed on the cavern floor below them, laughed, too.

"Buk," Kaslin said. The tar softened but still stuck.

The alien patted his head. "Bufu," it said. "Bufu bufu bufu." The tar lost its liquid quality and went back to being powdery and flaky.

They slipped down to the cavern floor in a flurry of flakes, ended up tangled together. Kaslin lay still, half buried in the floor, while the alien moved first one leg, then another, and separated from him. When it stood above him and held out a hand to pull him up, he rose with its help, and then he hugged its body, pressed his cheek against its chest, between all the shoulders where the many arms attached. Through its fur, its skin was hot and dry. It smelled like fallen leaves and fire.

It crooned.

Too late, he wondered if he were trespassing, doing something forbidden, something they'd kill him for. What did a croon mean?

Three of its arms wrapped around him, holding him against it. It rose on its other limbs and ran up the slope. "Beck beck," it murmured. He felt like an infant in a carrier. They reached the first plateau, and he waited for the alien to put him down, but it paused only a moment before carrying him across the flat part and becking its way up the next slide. The tunnel narrowed as they climbed; the soapy, waxy surface was only on the tunnel floor now instead of coating ceiling and walls. As the tunnel narrowed, the alien clutched him closer. There wasn't room for its legs to extend fully; it crept up the chimney/tunnel, its free limbs going all directions.

It stopped. They had reached the second plateau, just inside the cave, beyond the spread of the waxy coating. The alien lowered him to the ground. He saw a different light, a glow that had a harsh quality he was no longer used to.

The alien set him on his feet, then gave him a push in the back. He stumbled toward the light.

3

IT WAS NIGHT when he emerged into the spike tree grove. Starlight burned, sizzled against his skin, shocked his eyes. He was afraid of what the sun would do to him. The only upside to this new sensitivity was that he could see just fine, even though he knew it was night. Everything gave off a cool glow.

His new slick hairlessness was helpful; he slipped past trees and under spikes with ease. If Histly were chasing him now—

Histly.

He'd have to get help for her, whether he wanted to or not.

But first he needed a look in a mirror.

No one was at the house when he snuck home. The apartment was eerie in a new way: no lights had been left on, but he could see everything by the light of various clocks and displays on the entertainment tech in the group room, and the kitchen was visible by the light from just the screen, which had a message for him, and the phone and clock and weather lights. He checked the time and date on the kitchen chrono. How long had he been gone?

He'd entered the tunnel after school, around three in the

afternoon. Now it was three hours past midnight. Both his parents worked night shifts, his dad at the information center, his mother at the med lab; no one was home. His mother had left a glownote on the kitchen screen: *Kas, where are you? Call when you get home, no matter what time it is. Did you arrange to spend the night somewhere else and forget to tell us? If we don't hear from you before we get home, I'm raising hell!*

He headed for the phone, then passed it. No way was he going to call her on a vid line when he didn't even know what he looked like. She wasn't due home for another five hours. He could look at himself and then call, choose voice-only if he had to.

He tapped lights on in the bathroom. At first the glare made him flinch and cower. He cupped hands over his eyes and blinked rapidly. Was he going to need dark lenses for everyday life now?

He felt a shift, like a click on top his head just inside his skull. The light dimmed from blinding to pleasant. He dropped his hands and straightened, stared at his face in the mirror, then away. He looked like a ghost, pale and hairless. His lips had lost most of their color; his skin was more like snow than flesh, with faint blue rivers of veins in maplike traceries across it. Had this happened because he ate all those flakes? Had the aliens licked the color off his skin?

He stripped and stared at himself, difficult until he told himself he was looking at someone else. Hairless, he looked like a larva. His head was especially shocking. He'd always hidden behind his hair, which grew in thick and wavy, brown blond unless he streaked it, which he used to do on Hitherto. No one on Chuudoku streaked their hair, so he had stopped, though he still had supplies.

Like he'd need them now.

He guessed his skull was a decent shape. No obvious bumps. Still, no other Ash kid his age was totally bald. Most adults had full heads of hair. Bald was not a positive fashion statement here.

Then again, he had never been known for his fashion sense.

He dialed up a blood test, stuck his hand in the autodoc's slot, felt the needle slide through his skin and suck. Moments later, the med display lit up with unfamiliar colors and graphs. An alarm sounded. "Stay where you are. Help is on the way," said the autodoc.

That wasn't good. He wasn't ready to have anybody else see him. He'd be better off in the woods until he could figure out what was going on. He tried to pull his hand out of the slot. A wristlock dropped down and trapped him where he was.

"Don't panic," said the autodoc.

"Let go!" Kaslin tried to jerk loose, but the autodoc had him good. He hit buttons with his free hand, trying to manually override the 'doc, but it wouldn't respond.

He heard sirens; then he heard the apartment door open. Two people in biosuits rushed into the bathroom. One of them was his mother.

"Who are—Kaslin! Is that you? What happened to you? Where have you been?" she cried.

"Mom, I was going to call. I just wanted to go to the bathroom first."

"Son, are you all right? None of your blood values are normal," said the second biosuited person, a med tech named Avari who worked with his mother at the lab.

"I'd be fine if this stupid autodoc would let go of me."

His mother flipped up a panel on the wall and tapped some

sensidots, a code sequence. The wristlock released him. Kaslin grabbed his pants and pulled them on, embarrassed. He rubbed his wrist where the autodoc had gripped him. His skin felt smoother than it should. He lifted his hand to his nose and sniffed. A very faint odor of lemons.

Avari dialed up graphics on the autodoc's screen and studied them.

"Kaslin," said his mother, "please. Tell me what happened to you. Where'd your hair go?"

"What are all these unknown substances in your blood?" Avari asked. "How can you even be conscious?"

"I found this cave," Kaslin said. "There are aliens in it. I left Histly down there. I think I should probably go back for her."

"Aliens?" cried his mother.

"What kind of aliens? Bigger than lerts?" Lerts were small, many-limbed dog-sized omnivores, the largest animals anyone had seen on Chuudoku. Unfortunately, they didn't make good pets. They had poisoned spines, some of which had been the inspiration behind Histly's augmentations. They liked chewing on flesh. Their saliva was mildly narcotic, which led to some social problems until the med lab developed an aversive drug that the government supplied to all addicts, no protests allowed. The R&D lab worked up a synthetic version of the saliva drug for the offworld market. Most people shot lerts with tranquilizers if they showed up, because lerts were unfailingly bad-tempered. They could be kicked aside, though, if you wore tough enough boots; they didn't move quickly, and they weren't aggressive.

"Bigger than humans," said Kaslin. "They were nice to me. They fed me—" He dug a handful of flakes out of one of his pants' pockets. He touched his tongue to them. These were the bread flakes. He was hungry again. He bit off mouthfuls, sucked, chewed, swallowed.

"Stop it!" yelled his mother. "Don't you dare eat anything untested."

"Way too late for that."

Avari reached into a pocket of his biosuit and pulled out some specimen tubes. "Let me analyze it," he said.

Kaslin funneled some flakes into a tube, took another tube from Avari, and filled it with vinegar flakes from his other pocket. "This stuff is all over the network of tunnels I was in," he said. "There are lots of different tastes, but it mostly tasted good. I've been eating it for hours and it hasn't made me sick." He stared at his hand, turned it over so he could study the back of it. Paler than it had been, traced with veins, and, of course, no hair. "Not sick to my stomach, anyway. I don't know what happened to my skin."

"Let's get back to the aliens," said Avari. "Bigger than humans, you say? Did they speak?"

"Sure." He felt his head. "They said a lot of things, but I didn't learn many of the words. They ate all my hair off." He smoothed a finger along his browline. Nothing there but an angled edge of bone under the skin. He remembered the rasping touch of their tongues everywhere on him, moist and firm but not painful. Maybe there was something in their spit that dissolved hair, or their teeth were so sharp and accurate they had operated on him without his noticing. His hair must have tasted good to them; they had all wanted him. He shut down that train of thought, because he was getting aroused again.

"Ate your hair off?" His mother slid her gloved hand down

his arm, stroked his naked head. She hugged him, then pushed Avari away from the autodoc screen and punched buttons, viewed graphs, clicked her way through different displays. "Kas," she moaned.

"Am I sick? I feel all right."

"You're—"

Avari said, "I'm alerting the mayor. Somebody needs to decide what to do with this information. We might need a lockdown." He activated his wristphone. "And we probably need that dumb Cardy Hues from the Explorer's Bureau. I hate that woman. She's the local xenosociologist, though."

Kaslin's mother reached across and covered Avari's wristphone with her hand. "Wait, Avari. This is my son. Let's not alert anyone until we find out more."

Avari hesitated, then closed the phone aperture on his wrist. "Did these things have culture?"

"How do you define culture?" Kaslin asked.

"You should know this by now," said Avari. "Language. Tool use. Building. Higher purpose than subsisting."

"I don't know about all those things. They had language. They had these weird flakes, which might be a tool. I don't know about the building or the higher purpose."

"How many of them were there? Where'd they come from?"

"There were lots. I think they were hibernating in the wall until I woke them up."

"How many is lots?"

"I think I saw about twenty at one time. I don't know. There might have been more."

"We'll have to declare a state of emergency until we can define their status," Avari said.

Kaslin had participated in practice emergency response lockdown drills about once a month since he arrived. Nobody did things like that on Hitherto, but here on Chuudoku, at least in Ash, the powers that be weren't taking safety for granted. Chuudoku was a stealth planet, not on most maps. Its major industry was developing and exporting expensive, addictive drugs. Pirates had landed more than once trying to hijack shipments. They'd succeeded in intercepting drug shipments in space, but no one had stolen drugs on the planet. Chuudoku had an active augmented militia and a number of effective planetary defenses. They also had many creative uses for any person who broke the draconian planetary laws.

Kaslin had been at school the first time he heard an alert sound, a racket of whooping sirens. He hadn't known what was going on. Maya, one of his new neighbors in the partment complex where he lived and also a classmate, had explained it to him as everybody rose and lined up in front of the room. "It's a drill," she said. It was their first friendly contact.

"No talking," said the teacher.

"Follow me," said Maya. He followed her and the others, with Histly right behind him in line. They filed out and joined a silent, organized throng of other kids and teachers in the hall, then out into the yard to head into a blast-shielded shelter under the school.

He saw the dome shield spinning into being above the city. But he hadn't seen the inside of the shelter that time; it was the first time Histly poisoned him, dropping him into deep sleep on the playground.

He got in trouble for missing the drill. Nobody bothered to listen to his excuse until Maya backed him up. By the time they tested his blood, most of the sleep drug was gone, but there was enough left to identify Histly as the perpetrator. She got in much worse trouble, but it only made her mad. She'd zapped him with puke poison the next day.

Avari opened his phone again.

"Wait," said Kaslin's mother. "Please. Nothing immediate is happening. Let's find out more."

Avari frowned. "We're already violating six emergency laws."

"We can fix the record later. Not like we haven't done it before."

"Serena," said Avari, jerking his head toward Kaslin.

"It's family," said Kaslin's mother. "Remember your sister?"

Avari groaned and closed his phone.

Kaslin jumped up to sit on the bathroom counter, his back to the mirror. His mother took his hands in her gloved hands, stared down at his curled fingers.

"What is it, Mom? What's wrong with me?"

"I don't know yet, Kas. Your blood chemistry is screwy. There are still red and white blood cells in there, and they look fairly normal, but there are other substances, even other cells whose purposes I don't know. I don't have any alien profiles that match yours in my records, but you don't read as straight human anymore either."

"I think the food is some kind of machine." He dug the rest of the vinegar flakes out of his pocket. "Watch this." He spread the flakes across the surface of his hand in a layer. "Soft, right? Blook blook blook." He turned his hand over, dropped a hardened plate of flakes into his other hand. "Feel it."

She pinched the plate between gloved finger and thumb. "What?" she said.

"Buk buk buk," he whispered, and the flakes softened into snow texture again, drifted from between her fingers to rest on his open hand. "I ate them. I made things out of them. I walked on them and swam through them. They do different things. But once I ate them, they stopped working like this. I mean, I never got any hard lumps in my stomach, even when I was telling the stuff outside me what to do."

"Your stomach must have dissolved them. They're certainly in your bloodstream now, doing God knows what to your body." She rested a gloved hand on his chest, not pressing, but riding the rise and fall of his breathing. "You're conscious. You're thinking. Oriented in time and space. You can talk. No fever, no vomiting, no shakes. No spots. Strange skin condition," she muttered to herself, "but so far, not debilitating. What happened to you?"

She took a pinch of soft flakes from his hand and put them in the autodoc, punched the "analyze" button. The machine performed tests on the flakes, beeping to itself. She picked up another pinch of flakes, squashed them flat, and said, "Blook blook blook" to them. She dropped them on the counter. A white coin spanged off the counter and fell to the floor.

"Oych," she said. "The applications are—"

Kaslin balled the remaining flakes. "Watch this." He murmured, "Bink bink bink," and pink glow blossomed in his hand. "Beck." He dipped a finger in the glow, and the pink stuck; when he lifted the finger, a strand of pink dragged up with it, gleaming as though wet. "Bufu." The strand collapsed in a drift of pink light. "Bsstu bsstu bsstu." The light went out.

"Favo," said Avari. "Fantastic! There's more? Glad you stopped me from calling this in. If only we could patent it, Serena, before the gov gets it. Kas, you have to come to the lab, let us observe you for a while so we can find out what the side effects and aftereffects are."

"I have to?" He looked at his mother.

Through her hood, he saw her eyes cloud. Her brows rose at the inner edges. He saw the moment when he turned from her son into data, a walking test subject. Saw the flicker as she reversed the transformation and turned him back into her son. She clenched her hands in front of her.

"I need a drink of water," he said, and left, before they could remind him that there was water in the bathroom tap. He paused in the kitchen and turned on a tap, then dashed out the door into what was left of the night.

There were trackers that could see footsteps for an hour or two after a person left them, just by the temperature residue left behind. There were forensic devices that could find traces of passage at a molecular level. Nobody got lost on Chuudoku, at least not forever. Not so far.

Nobody got lost, and nobody successfully snuck in; there were satellites monitoring planet activity all the time, and a team of watchers who kept track of everything the satellites picked up. His father was on the code-writing team that fine-tuned the satellite search parameters to rule out ordinary activity versus suspicious activity.

Nobody had sent out a search team after him and Histly yet. If they had, the cave would have already been discovered; it would be swarming with techs and equipment.

Still, he wanted to go somewhere else this time and lead people away from the cave. He didn't want to make it easy for anybody to find the aliens. So he headed away from the spike tree grove and toward the Salton Sea.

There was an outpost of Ash on the sea, a distillery that refined fresh water and various kinds of minerals and salts from the ocean water. He'd been on a field trip there with his edsection. There was a different kind of forest by the water, scaly-trunked trees with feather bursts of leaves at their tops, and harsh-stemmed vines that wound around them in strangles and loops, loaded with agile flowers that shot seeds into passing animals, activated by the change in heat between a living thing and ambient temperature.

The seeds were opportunists that took root in whatever flesh they landed in; the seedlings lived on the host animals for a while before they dropped off onto suitable soil. Humans weren't their preferred hosts, but early experiences had taught both plants and people that humans could be used. The foreign flesh only mildly warped the seeds' usual growth patterns and the metamorphoses of the infant plants. The humans, after initial unpleasant immune-system responses to the invasion, grew accustomed to plant parasitism, even addicted to it.

People who had been colonized ran to the forest again as soon as they had lost their seedlings, anxious for another encounter with the armed flowers. Another reason the gov didn't eradicate these trees. The particular form of intoxication practiced by the plants didn't impede the host's ability to work; it kept its users placid, hungrier than usual (they were eating for themselves and their colonizers), more cautious about avoiding danger. The seedlings' drugs increased stamina and the ability to endure long hours of boring work without complaint. Kaslin had never paid much attention to work groups outside school and his house; he had seen some people who had plants living on them, but he hadn't studied them. He'd heard other kids muttering about mossybacks. The colonized did boring work like garbage pickup, gardening, basic manufacturing. The small forests on their backs grew from their butts all the way up into their hair, like green horse manes.

On the field trip, the teachers had kept the kids far from this forest.

Kaslin ran on the road toward the distillery, figuring he probably wouldn't leave tracks on the pavement, even though he was barefoot, since he had run away from home with nothing but pants on. If they came after him right away, there would be no disguising the heat signature of his footprints. If they waited—maybe Mom would wait. Maybe she wouldn't. Avari probably wouldn't, unless Mom could play on his cupidity, convince him that keeping Kaslin a secret might benefit them both in the long run.

Kaslin thought about his father, off herding data. Was Dad searching for him now, using all the equipment at his command? Maybe, if somebody prodded him into it. Dad kept making choices that got them deeper and deeper into trouble. He was smart, but used his smarts for dumb things, like figuring out how to fool gambling machines on Hitherto. The casino bosses had been impressed with the way he got around all their protections. One of the big casinos had offered Dad a job in security. He'd had that job about three months before he lost it by figuring out ways to siphon money out of accounts he was supposed to be protecting. Next thing they knew, it was prison or get off the planet.

If only Dad had figured out how to be a successful crook. He had no idea how to be a good father, either. When Kaslin had first complained about what Histly was doing to him, Dad had said, "Stop running away. Just stand there and let her do her worst until she gets bored. She'll leave you alone and move on to someone more fun soon enough. Your mom has good insurance. The gov should take care of any medical problems you get from the way the girl treats you."

Dad hadn't spent hours puking uncontrollably. Kaslin suspected Histly's other poisons would be even worse. But maybe she'd used the meanest things in her repertoire first. He really needed to hack into the med records.

Provided he was loose, not trapped in the med center himself.

Or maybe he didn't have to worry about Histly anymore. She could just stay lost underground forever.

On the other hand, the aliens had released him. Why wouldn't they let Histly go, too?

He'd have to go back and try to get her out, no matter how mean she was. Or maybe she liked it down there? He kind of liked it. He would have gone back if he could have done it without leading other humans to the cave.

He wondered if Histly's parents were worried about her. Maybe they were glad she was gone. Maybe her little sister, Fidi, also augmented but less inclined to use her special skills against her classmates, was glad. Kaslin was in an after-school gaming club with Fidi. He liked her. He suspected she had spent some time puking, too.

A quiet motor sounded on the trail behind him. Kaslin glanced over his shoulder. Off in the distance, he saw the green headlight of one of the small personal transport scooters. Not exactly a full-scale-alert-capture-the-prisoner vehicle. It was probably just somebody going on shift at the distillery. Better if he didn't see Kaslin, though. Where could Kaslin hide?

This was a stupid plan, going to the ocean. He didn't have many choices of hiding places. The water in its natural state was inimical to human life; if you fell in, the high concentration of salts and minerals in the water made osmosis drain fluids out of your body and left you desiccated in minutes. The snake tree and assassin vine forest was scary, and the distillery, though mainly automated, was under observation, just like every other key place on the planet.

He needed a place to duck. The forest was the only cover. He sighed and headed for the snake trees and their wreaths of vines. Maybe the flowers closed at night.

He picked his way between two snake trees that were less wrapped in vines than others and ducked down behind the one with the thicker trunk. Maybe the scooter would pass by.

It was trundling slowly, wobbling back and forth on the road, and a strange sound came from its rider over the quiet hum of the electric motor. It took Kas a while to recognize the noise as singing. He clutched the tree trunk. When his hand touched its bark, a slide of overlapping scales like shingles, he heard rustling behind him. He turned. One of the vines eeled toward him, four flowers facing him as though they were seeking eyes.

He knew the plants could aim; the infovids had said as much. He hadn't realized they could move like snakes.

He turned away and shut his eyes, waiting for the burrow of armed seeds into his naked back.

Thin snaky things brushed over his cheek, his chest, his shoulders. Something softer brushed his forehead. Something curled around his arms, and then there was a frenzy of rustling and wrapping. He had to open his eyes to see what was happening, ready to blink them shut if any of the flowers was staring his way. A burrowing seed in his eye? The idea made him shiver.

The vines webbed him in a half-cocoon. Flowers hung near his face, their scents strong and strange, an acid/sweet combination that tingled in his nose and on his tongue. None of the flowers were aimed at him, though the one above his forehead dusted yellow-orange pollen on his nose. It sizzled on his skin but didn't burn him.

"Too-rah loo-rah loo-rah," sang the person on the scooter. He fell off right in front of the tree Kaslin hid behind. "Too-rah loo-rah lai." The fall didn't seem to have hurt him much. He kept singing while flat on his back. "Too-rah, loo-rah, loo-rah, that's an Islish lullaby."

The vines rustled across Kaslin's back. It felt like they were concentrating there, growing more dense. Something poked at the edge of his mouth. He clamped his lips and teeth shut, but something slipped in anyway, like a finger, feeling along the outside of his clenched teeth, probing until it wound around his molars and touched his tongue.

Vinegar, like the flakes in his pocket.

No infovids about this. The plants acting so weird, and him afraid to move because the drunk singer in the road might notice him. Should he bite off the thing in his mouth? Yeah, and make all the rest of the plants mad?

"Too-rah, loo-rah, what are you doing in the bushes, boy?" The man writhed around a moment, then sat up.

"What?" Kaslin said, forgetting he was hiding out from the plants and their pushiness. The instant he opened his mouth, one of the flowers near his chin turned and lobbed a seed between his teeth. An explosion of hot across his tongue, a conflagration in his mouth, fever all through him, and the plants, agitated as he jerked and struggled. Then a cascade of cool. Spit filled his mouth. He swallowed, felt the burning, freezing seed slide down his throat.

Okay, this was good, he could die of plant poison, twisted up in a plant embrace out by the ocean.

Or maybe not. Once the seed hit his stomach, the fever went away. Calm flowed through him.

Not assassin vine behavior at all. Putting a seed in his mouth, letting him swallow it down into his stomach, where his stomach acid had probably already dissolved it. What was the point of that? And there was a point—the plants' actions had been deliberate. They wanted something from him. Or maybe they wanted him tranquil? Unconscious? He was ready to be unconscious, especially if it were someone else's choice so he didn't have to take the blame for it. He felt like he'd been running away from various threats for hours.

The plants on his back shifted around, baring most of it, winding tighter around his arms and sides. They gripped his neck from the sides, and framed his face the way his hairline used to, leaving most of his scalp and the back of his neck bare. He felt odd, tightly constrained and naked at the same time.

He was almost asleep when a flurry of bullets hit his head, neck, and back. There was a sheet of stinging over his back, and then subsidence.

4

"WHAT?" he muttered again, his tongue still tingling from seed burn.

Small arrows of pain darted into his back here and there, three of them in the back of his neck, a scattering across his head.

The vine cocoon the plants had woven around him relaxed. The vines dropped in loose loops around his feet. He ran his hands over his bare head, felt a scattering of bumps. He prodded one and was rewarded with a burst of pain and a little wet. He looked at his finger. Blood.

So the seeds had landed and burrowed. That was normal assassin vine behavior. Maybe everybody who was colonized got a seed in the mouth, and they'd just neglected to mention it to the people who made the infovids. It would make sense to immobilize your prey before you used it as an incubator.

Two hundred years of colonization and reverse colonization; you'd think somebody would have mentioned a thing like that.

A throb of sensation shivered across his back. Then another. Then a sputter under his skin, the purr of some little motor or a happy animal.

Suddenly he felt better. Euphoric.

Maya had told him about assassin vine highs while they were on a field trip at the Museum of Native Traces. She had a friend who was an assassin vine partner. Her friend had told her that being a plant host was like having the TV on all the time. He saw visions of stories and plays, and they made him happy. If he didn't like the direction a story was going, he could switch it by thinking at it. Mostly he watched porn.

"Kid?"

Kaslin licked his lips and waited for the TV in his head to switch on. It didn't happen. Well, maybe he should disregard other people's stories about what was going to happen to him, because he was already too different to act like other people. He felt good. His back, neck, and scalp glowed with a pleasing warmth. He felt an under-the-skin movement.

"Kid? Come on out. I'm not going to hurt you. It's just me, old Dilly, on my way to my shift at the plant. I didn't mean to chase you into the woods."

Old Dilly? Kaslin didn't know him. He guessed he didn't have to be afraid of the forest anymore, now that he was colonized; he could ease in among the trees. Or he could come out and show his new seed sites. That couldn't end well. The colonized were sent to the med center to be monitored until the doctors knew they were under control of the seedlings, at which point they were assigned the jobs no one else wanted. Now that Kaslin thought about it, he realized that the colonized were a resource.

"I won't send you to the center," said Dilly. "It's not in the common literature, but if you get those seeds off you in the first hour, you can avoid being a plant host. I've got a scalpel out at the distillery. I've used it on people before. What are you running away from, kid?"

Dilly looked old and fat. Kaslin was sure he could run away from Dilly if push came to shove. He slid between the trees back out to the road, maintained a two-meter distance between himself and Dilly, who was a large, cheery-looking guy with a wide mouth, smiling now, and feathers of light hair around his face. Dilly wore a blue worksuit and a utility belt hung with tools and a communicator. Using the scooter for a crutch, he struggled to his feet, then righted the scooter.

"Hi, there, kid. You really bald? You're sure pale," Dilly said. "Are you an albino?"

"No," said Kaslin.

"Turn around. Let me see your infestation."

Kaslin turned, poised to run if Dilly approached him. Chuudoku cops had tanglecuffs they could toss at people they considered criminals. The cuffs would wrap around the suspects, bring wrists and ankles together, like hog-tying a calf in infovids about the Old West on Earth. If Dilly carried cuffs and wanted to use them, Kaslin was wide open for an attack. He waited.

"They must love you," Dilly said. "I count thirty-three separate seed sites. Want me to cut 'em out?"

"I don't know. Have you ever been colonized?"

"Used to do it regular. Fine work for a guy with no ambition." Dilly's footsteps came closer on the packed shell road. "Most they ever shot me with was about eighteen, though. The plants knew my tolerance pretty well. Eighteen was a lot. Kept me too dopey to do anything but manual. Mostly I managed about fifteen of them. At that rate, I could keyboard if I didn't have to think."

"Did they shoot one in your mouth first?"

"What? They do that to you? Wonder what that's about? Doesn't sound productive. Hostile environment, the mouth. Also, it's just plain disgusting. What if it roots on your tongue? Might keep you from talking. Wouldn't keep you from signaling or keyboarding, though. And anyway, that's not the plan, since you're talking all right. Let me see inside your mouth."

"I swallowed it," Kaslin said.

"Weird. Might make 'em mad. Hard to tell. I don't know if they think or have feelings. They ought to run on instinct, same as other Chuudoku critters. Dang. I'm sorry I scared you into there, kid. This many babies, you're going to be way too dumb to do anything."

"How long does it take for them to grow up and drop off?"

"Standard colonization time's about three months. You got a support system? Somebody's gonna have to buy your food, and you're going to be eating three times as much as you used to. Maybe four times."

Kaslin thought of the caverns full of food/light/tools/waxy flakes. It hadn't been twenty-four hours since his first bite, though, and he didn't know yet if the food was nutritious enough to support him. His body hadn't told him it was hungry for anything but more of the cavern stuff.

If he went home, Mom and Dad could probably support an amplified food habit. They were doing well on Chuudoku. Mom had joined citizen committees, and she seemed to be leaning toward politics and favors. On the other hand, she might feel it was her responsibility to the colony to turn him in for testing and dissection. In addition to testing him for alien alterations.

His best bet was probably to go underground.

"Let me cut at least some of those suckers out, or you're going to be miserable, maybe sick. I remember one time a kid got too many plants on him and they had to stick him on an IV to support them all. Once they sprout, you can't take 'em off; they'll poison you rather than let you pull 'em."

"Okay." Kaslin tried to catch up with everything that had happened to him. Yesterday he'd just been a kid in school with bully problems.

"Come on out to the plant with me. Hide around the side while my coworker leaves, and then I'll get you in there and go at them. Okay?"

"Okay. Thanks, Dilly."

Dilly walked his scooter, and Kaslin strolled beside him, conscious of the glow and purring from his back. "What were you doing out this road anyway?" Dilly asked.

"Running away."

"Yeah, I got that. What's such a big problem you volunteer to be infested instead of facing it?"

"I can't really talk about it."

Dilly shrugged, but he looked hurt.

Anything Kaslin told him would just make trouble, he figured.

The seedthrum on his back hummed higher, as though his back, neck, and head were strings being swept into melody. He stopped, sensed motion over his back and head, an itch that scratched itself. He lifted a hand, placed it palm down over some of the seed sites on his head. They squirmed under his palm, damp again with warm liquid. Pinpoints prickled against his palm and fingers. The seeds were sprouting.

"Whoa," said Dilly. He backed up and was staring at the

seething on Kaslin's back. "Fast. Way too fast. They're sprouting already! That means the roots found your bloodstream, and they've loaded up the poison nodules. Those'll burst if I try anything. Too late to cut 'em out now. What are you, some kind of mutant?"

"I guess," Kaslin said.

"Should probably send you to the center at this point. The planties are going to suck you dry so fast you'll faint. They're hungriest right at the start; that's when they grow fastest. Want me to call you an ambulance?"

"No!"

"Running away's not the answer with an infestation like yours. You play your cards right, the gov will pay for your care. They're going to want to study your mutant ass."

"I know."

"You don't get help, kid, you'll be killing yourself one way or another. Pull the seedlings out, they'll poison you. Leave 'em in, they'll suck you down to nothing and drug you out of your mind until you forget to eat. I don't think you can tough it out."

"I need to get to this place I know," Kaslin said, despairing. He wasn't sure how to get around the authorities either. Already waves of happiness rolled over him, and hunger gnawed his gut. The squirming and flopping of the seedlings on his back, neck, and head felt strange, but again, arousing. A taste of chocolate rested on his tongue. He realized he loved the presence of the plants on his back, and realized that this love was probably sent to him from the plants.

He dug the last handful of bread flakes out of his pocket, crammed them into his mouth. As soon as they dissolved on his tongue, the plants on his back surged with an almost electric power.

"What did you just do?" Dilly asked. "Your plants are way too wild! They're in second leaf already. What did you eat?"

A whee-woo whee-woo alarm sounded on the road back toward Ash.

"Might as well wait for them to get you, kid," Dilly said. He stirred a finger through the growth on Kaslin's back. "There's no exit off this road except into the assassin vines, or into the water, and you don't want that. Let the gov get you; they'll take care of you. They like information more than anything else, and you're probably crawling with it."

"I need—I need…" His stomach was a gaping maw, crying for more. His brain was drifting away on clouds of silly happiness. The rustling on his head pleased him. He patted his scalp, felt the baby forest up there. Not bald anymore. Good.

Dilly caught him as he swayed and fell, eased him facedown onto the white road. The siren got louder. Kaslin dreamed of the caves again, where he was surrounded by food and giant spiders who could carry him around. "Buk buk," he whispered, longing for ground that would open and swallow him, aching for flaky white stuff to shovel into his mouth and ease the hunger.

The ambulance pulled up beside him, glitterlight flashing. The alarm had been switched off. Two people in biosuits jumped out. "Oh, Kas," said his mother, kneeling beside him.

"Sorry," he said.

"Ma'am, he needs nourishment right away. His colony's crazy fast," Dilly said.

Avari squatted beside him, shone a light over his back; he could follow its passage by the feel of the action of the plants, which quivered as light touched them. "If I hadn't seen him two hours ago, I would say this colony was at least two weeks old," Avari muttered.

"Mom? I need to get back to the cavern."

"The cavern?"

"Where the white stuff is. Where the aliens are. I think I'll be all right if I can get there."

"Meantime, eat this, Kas," said Avari. He pulled a foodblock out of a pocket of his biosuit, touched the unzip to pop it out of its cover and set it warming.

Kaslin propped himself on his elbows and wolfed the bar. It had no flavor and no texture, no crunch. It slid down his throat easily, soothed the scream of his stomach a little. He reached for more, and Avari gave him three in a row. "That's all I got, kid."

"There's more in the ambulance," said his mother. She knelt beside him, took his hand, dragged him to his feet. "Come on."

Once he was inside the government vehicle, would he ever get out in freedom again? Avari gripped his other arm. Kaslin wasn't sure he could break away from them, and he was tired and still hungry, anyway. He walked toward the ambulance with them, turned to call over his shoulder, "Thanks for your help, Dilly."

"Sorry I wasn't faster, kid. This gov woman really your mother?"

"Yeah."

"Sorry again. You take care, kid. Let me know how it comes out."

In the ambulance, Avari strapped him facedown to the med table. He was too surprised to fight. "What's this?" he asked.

"First thing we have to do is take out your locator," said his mother.

"I have a locator?"

"Sure. We all got them on arrival. I don't know if you've noticed this, Kas, but Chuudoku is a very paranoid planet." She rubbed some icy-hot liquid over his upper shoulder, which, come to think of it, had developed a red bump that stung for a week after he arrived. He had thought it was a bug bite.

She used an extractor, plucked a tiny gory thing from under his skin, dropped it into a jar full of red jelly and small devices. "Now this is the official you," she said. She capped the jar and touched some sensidots on it. Telltales flickered to life on the jar's graphscreen.

"Where are we going?" Avari asked from the driver's seat.

"We should leave Official Kaslin at the med center," said his mother.

"Oh, right." The vehicle hummed into movement.

"Kaslin, foodblock or drip?" asked his mother.

"Foodblock," he said.

She opened a cupboard and got down a sixpack of foodblock. She sat in the paramedic's seat beside him and fed him foodblock as Avari navigated the morning streets of Ash.

Kaslin felt strange. Flickers of memory, his mother feeding him when he was too young to feed himself, spoonfuls of hot cereal with sweetening, the songs she'd sing to get him to open his mouth. He felt like a baby bird. The plants hummed with warmth on his back, rustling in the light of the ambulance. He felt like he lay under a heavy, warm blanket that could purr.

Where was the TV-in-his-head thing that Maya had promised him? If he'd go under like that, he could make it so nothing mattered. He would be at the mercy of forces beyond his control. Yeah. What a plan.

The ambulance whirred to a stop. Avari reached back and Mom handed him the Official Kaslin. "Any recs on where to lodge it?"

"Under an empty bed on the third floor. Maybe you should check him in. Here's his card." Mom rummaged through something and pulled out Kaslin's ID. She had his toolbelt. Avoz! He'd left it in the bathroom at home when he stripped to look at himself.

Avari vanished. Mom fed Kaslin more foodblock. The hunger in his stomach quieted, but no vids started in his head.

He was, however, getting some kind of soundtrack. It wasn't in any language he recognized. The instruments were wind, a gentle mingling of soft breezes in different pitches.

Were the plants singing?

"Mom? Do you hear that?"

"Hear what?"

"Music?"

"No, Kas. But it's all right. Perfectly normal. People usually hallucinate when they're colonized."

"It's not visual."

"Auditory hallucinations are common. I've got a friend who's studying hallucination content in the colonized. She's got theories about where people's minds go under the influence of assassin plants—something about returning to periods of less stress. I can't remember any time when we weren't stressed to the max, until we got here. What kind of music do you hear?"

"Nothing I've heard before."

"That's not typical," she muttered. "They should be pinging your memories for content."

The front door opened and Avari climbed back into the driver's seat. "He's checked into bed three forty-three," he said. "Now where?"

"Kas, how do we get to your cavern?"

"You guys are going AWOL? What about your locators?"

"I hacked into the feed. I'm going to supply false locations as soon as we leave our beaten track," said Avari. He checked his wrist for the time. "Now that we've delivered you to the med center and our emergency job is up, we should head home." He got out a pinpad and worked the sensidots on it. "There. We're on our way. Soon we'll be home eating breakfast. Kas? How do we get to your cavern?"

"There's a spike tree grove to the west of school...."

They left the ambulance in the school parking lot and made their way through the forest. The spike tree grove looked impenetrable and strange. Kaslin felt a warm spot in his stomach that pulled him toward the hole in the ground he had come out of during the night. With the lively plants on his back, he had trouble getting through the spikes. Avari had a small laser; once they had worked their way far enough into the forest, with Serena doing something to cover their trail by laying down heat-deadening dust, Avari clipped leaves and branches so Kaslin could follow his stomach.

The cavern mouth was farther away than he had thought, and looked much smaller than he remembered. How had the alien carried him up out of it? It hadn't come all the way to the end. Kas remembered how fierce the light had been, even from far back inside. And that was from the night sky. Now that it was morning—no, he was seeing with normal eyes.

He looked around. Spike trees, the litter of shed spikes below them, some viny tangles in the upper canopies, and beyond, a blue sky with a feather fan of thin clouds to the east. To the north, the Carcinoma Mountain Range showed above the tree tops. Thin slivers of city were visible through the trees to the east. The cavern entrance wasn't far from Ash. How had it gone unnoticed all this time? Other kids must have run through this grove from bullies in their time. Let alone the gov did massive surveys of anywhere they planned to settle a city; they scanned for all kinds of resources. Had the ground slumped, opening this hole recently?

He was no geologist. He couldn't tell. Maybe someone would work it out later.

Kaslin lowered himself carefully to his stomach and elbowed his way into the entrance.

"Kas?"

"Come on if you're coming," Kaslin said. The cavern opened up inside and he sat up, then crawled forward on hands and knees.

It was dark in here. He blinked quickly and his eyes shifted, opened to enhanced sight. The wax floor was near. He plunged forward, got his hands on it, muttered, "Buk buk buk," and felt it go powdery. He shoveled handfuls into his mouth. Wall polish and burnt sugar, undertone of lemon. Blech! But it fed the second hunger in his stomach. The vines on his back surged and rustled.

Avari in his biosuit was too big to get in through the opening, but Mom managed to squeeze inside. She flicked on a light in her helmet. Kas closed his eyes against the brilliance. He elbowed himself forward onto the wax. Before he could speak it soft, he was sliding down again, irresistibly shooting down the first long slope. He didn't even try to stop himself, just made sure he stayed facedown so the plants on his back were safe.

"Beck beck beck," he muttered as the ground leveled and he shot across the first plateau. The ground turned sticky. Eventually he stopped, caught in a morass of tarlike white stuff. He plunged his face into it and ate. Not a successful experiment; it gummed his mouth up. He could barely buk it into powder. Once he swallowed it, he said, "Bufu bufu bufu!" The stickiness subsided into slick surface again.

He sat up, bukked at the floor, and ate. The flakes here tasted like filufa fruit, a Hitherto native he'd never liked until now. The plants on him rustled and grew, trailing vines over his shoulders, sprays of small arrowhead leaves dripping down his front and over his upper arms. The plants' leaves weren't green, but pale fleshy purple in the faint pink light. The vines on his head dangled down before his face. Where the plants had rooted, his skin felt hot and strange, meshed. The stems were thick as his fingers, with soft spikes sprouting at the base of each leaf stem. He was growing his own thicket, and all he wanted was to make it bigger. He pulled himself across the floor with his fingers, bukking up more floor and swallowing it.

"Bink bink bink," said someone else.

Light bloomed. Rustling sounds came from the chute. Kaslin paused in his quest to stuff himself full of flakes and glanced up to see one of the aliens peering down at him. It lifted a flower-hand, parted the vines over his face, touched his cheek. "Bootah bistu bilia," it said.

"Bootah," said Kas, still not sure what he was talking about.

His mother slid out of the chute and shot across the floor,

heading right for him and the alien.

"Bike!" said the alien. The floor rose up in a bubble and trapped her.

"*Oof*," she said, and fought free of it, shedding big, stretchy sheets of white stuff. "Kaslin?"

The alien grasped his arms and lifted him to his feet, turned him to face his mother.

A thudding, thumping symphony came from the chute, and then Avari shot out, collided with Serena and knocked her down. "Bike," cried the alien. The floor ballooned to encompass and stop both of them.

"Bik lilia bootah bishona nik," the alien told Kaslin.

"I'm sorry. I didn't know what else to do. These plants. I was hungry. I'm sorry."

"Negev." It ran hands down his arms, his front. It didn't sound mad. Then again, he didn't know anything about its emotional landscape, or what tone of voice meant to it. How could he judge?

The alien lifted three hands to stroke through the plants sprouting from Kaslin's back. The plants were exuberant, almost noisy in their growth. Faint strains of wind music continued under the sound of his mother and Avari fighting through their white bubble.

"Biki nik nenuma," said the alien. It leaned forward and licked Kaslin's cheek between the fronds of his personal forest. Kaslin shivered, memory flashing to the last time one of them had licked him. This one straightened, though, and he calmed himself.

Avari and Mom broke free. Avari's suit had split. He sighed and pulled off his helmet, collapsed it, and shoved it into one of his cargo pockets. "So I guess I'm in the First Contact lottery now," he muttered, then looked up and saw the alien beside Kas. "Flitch!"

"Mom. Avari. This is—" Kaslin turned and looked up at the alien. He didn't know its name. They'd never introduced themselves. Did he even know which one this was? It reached a casual hand over and pressed it to his chest, the fuzzy bristles on its rays of fingers a pleasant friction. "One of the aliens," he said. The hand slid down across his stomach. He caught and stopped it before it could open his pants. There was so much they hadn't talked about. So many subjects he hadn't even considered discussing, like alien manners in front of one's mother.

Four more aliens materialized from the shadows and approached Mom and Avari. "Bootah bootah," they murmured. Two of them explored Avari with their hands, leaned forward to lick him.

"Bootah?" Mom said.

"Bootah!" all the aliens answered.

"Hey!" Avari yelled as one took a bite of his hair. He struggled, and they immobilized him by grasping his wrists and ankles and pulling to extend his arms and legs out straight so he hung between them like a muscular star. "Hey! Hey! Stop it!" A third joined the first two and cradled his head in its palm, raising it on a plane with his body so he was flat, parallel to the floor, and helpless. They stopped licking him to study him visually. The fourth stroked its hands over Serena's biosuit.

"Kas?" she said.

He ran over to them, pulling the alien by the hand he still held. "It's all right," he said. "Or maybe it's not. This is what they do. They want to taste you."

The alien Kaslin had dragged over added its hands to the exploration of Avari. It reached inside his suit, loosened stiktites, skinned him out of it. It murmured to the others, and they murmured back. Various hands reached back to tap Kaslin's chest, stomach, shoulder, to finger his new growths.

"Kas!" his mother yelled. More and more aliens arrived to cluster around them, and one of them found the stiktites on his mother's suit and, despite her frantic struggles to stop them, stripped her out of it. They held her the same way they were holding Avari.

"Hey," Kaslin said as they worked Avari and Mom out of the clothes they wore under the biosuits. "Hey, don't." He had visualized this encounter a lot differently. The aliens and Avari and Mom would meet, stare at each other across space, speak. Mom would have a translator program running that would pin down alien grammar and vocabulary. Maybe they would all shake hands and sign a treaty.

Not this. This was what happened to kids who didn't know any better, not to adults who had come armed and always knew what to do in tough situations. Avari was augmented. Why wasn't he deploying his personal protections? The aliens wouldn't let him move, that was why. They held and stroked and licked him, now that they'd skinned him out of his clothes, and Kas could see that Avari liked it the same way Kas had. "Flitch," Avari muttered, jerking in their hold, but not because he was trying to get away.

"Kas," said his mother in her dangerous voice. "Make them stop."

Kaslin tugged on alien hands and arms, tried to pull them

away from his mother. "Stop it. Please. Don't. Leave her alone, okay?"

They patted him where the plants didn't cover him, and pushed him out of the circle surrounding his mother.

"Stop it," he said again, grabbing spider legs and shaking. Strokes and gentle pushes were all he got in response. "Mom?" he yelled through the brown, hairy forest of legs. "I can't get them to stop."

"All right," she said, her voice tight and strange.

He leaned his forehead against a leg. The plants shifted, hot, wet, and digging into him, across his back, and his stomach roared with hunger. He turned and ran.

He came to the edge of the second plateau and stared down the slope into darkness. He couldn't watch them do to his mother what they had done to him. He didn't understand the vocabulary enough to order the aliens around, and he had no idea if they'd listen to him, anyway, even if he begged them to stop. His stomach growled. He had come here for food. That was his job: feed these plants on his back so he could get rid of them. His mouth was so dry. He was thirsty, and so was his forest. He remembered there were lakes in the cavern below.

He eased onto his stomach and pulled himself over the edge.

A pile of stirred-up powder stopped him after the long slide. He sat up and grabbed a handful, bit it. Blech, motor oil! He spat out what he could. "Bink bink bink." Light showed him scuffs and scars in the floor, tracks where he and Histly and maybe the aliens had come much earlier. He stood up, took two steps, and sank into the floor.

"Blook," he said. He blooked his way across the floor to one of the dips where water lay, then eased down and stuck his face into it, swallowing as quickly as he could. The water was cold and tasted clean. His back was alive with rustling plants now, heavier than they had been, far too kinetic. He felt the roots like hot wires in his skin and muscles, pushing farther into him, sucking moisture out of him faster than he could drink it down. All the while, though, he felt euphoria mixed with the pain. The plants were ecstatic—happy, especially, with him and all he was doing for them.

He used his elbows to lever himself into the pool. If there was any way to get water into himself faster, he wanted to find it.

The cold of the water soothed him. The mesh of burning wires under the skin of his scalp, neck, and back cooled after he got into the pool. The water wasn't deep enough for him to get all the way under, but with him flat on his stomach, it came up almost even with his back, and he could still drink and breathe. He drank, and the forest on his back grew, sent out shoots and tendrils that knotted and meshed with each other, leaves and more shoots, a thick blanket of foliage, growing denser so fast he could feel it. He drank, and the plants sent out their own roots to drink, too. The plants fed him contentment and joy.

Eventually his throat didn't parch the moment he stopped drinking to breathe. He pushed up out of the water, managed to get to his knees, though his back and neck didn't bend anymore. His stomach growled. He scooted to the edge of the pond. "Buk buk buk," he muttered to the beach, and ate some. Grilled meat with salt and juices. Still sitting in the water, he shoveled white powder into his mouth and swallowed and tried not to think about this being his existence for the foreseeable future. Three months of this? Three months?

Long brown shoots came down from the plants on his head, not stems or leaves but things that looked like endless fingers, or really fat hairs. Only a few hung down at first, then more and more. He wanted to look over his shoulder to see if brown things were sticking out from the main mass of his forest, but he couldn't turn his head, and his stomach still cried for more food. The wire lace of roots in his back didn't burn him anymore, but he felt occasional flexes and sparks, small jolts he interpreted as pleasure.

The brown fingers grew long enough to touch the ground. After the first batch did it, all the others, which had been waving round his head, aimed groundward and plunged through the soft surface of the cavern floor. He was webbed to the ground. He had just enough time to wonder if they'd drag him down and lock him to the floor before the first plant popped free of his scalp, and, using its walking roots, swayed over the ground away from him.

Then came a cascade of pops and some determined untangling. They pulled up all the roots they'd used to anchor themselves in his back, and staggered off in all directions, waving tendrils in the air like feelers, swaying along on many long, brown, spindly roots, like baby spiders finding their feet. The last one pulled up roots and walked up his back, stopped on his head and wrapped its walking roots under his chin. It didn't plunge regular roots into his scalp.

His back felt cold and naked with all of them gone. A breeze he hadn't noticed before wisped over the holes in his flesh. He turned his head—finally a skill he could reclaim—but he still couldn't see his own back. He put a hand to the back of his neck. Three pits in it big enough for the tip of his little finger to dig into, but no real pain. He checked his hand. No blood on his fingertip. They had sealed him up enough so that he wasn't leaking, anyway. How could people do this more than once? How could they endure it for three months? The euphoria had made it easier, sure, but it wasn't so wonderful he wanted to go to a grove of assassin vines again and bare his back to them.

He rolled over onto his back, something else he had anticipated not being able to do for a long while yet, though occasional grim fantasies of rolling over on the baby plants had flickered through his mind. As he rolled, the one plant still on his head scraped its walking roots over his face and neck to steady itself, but refused to drop off. It didn't have any roots in his skin anymore. Maybe he could force it off and not get poisoned.

He harbored a strange, sneaking fondness for it, though. The little plants had turned him into an eating and drinking machine for their convenience, but he sort of liked that. They were just doing what they always did, what they had to do to live. It had felt good to have a purpose—to help something that needed it. He had raised them all; they were his children, even against his will. Maybe he could keep one for a pet, see if it turned out okay.

He was crazy. He should be mad at them. Should want to take a flamethrower back to the parent grove and shoot them all up. Thirty-three seed sites. Flesh-eating plants. That, after being examined minutely by a new kind of alien. First Contact lottery, Avari had called it. Why him? Why Histly, for that matter?

What was he complaining about? His dream had come true, even if he'd blown it. He'd made first contact. How many people could say that?

The soft, feathery floor against his back soothed the remnants of burn away. He could pack his new pits with white stuff, look like some kind of spotted animal from a vid. Bound to make him more popular at school. Sure. That, plus the whole-body baldness and whatever had turned him ghost white instead of the tan his skin normally was. Hey, maybe the pits in his back would be invisible if he camouflaged them with floor-stuff. Maybe no one at school would notice. Assuming he ever got back to school, instead of being cooped up at the med center or sent to jail for—for what? Had he actually committed any crimes?

He'd left Histly down here. Maybe he should get up and look for her. How hard could it be? She was probably still cursing and screaming somewhere.

It occurred to him he was exhausted. He swallowed a last mouthful of flakes, laid his head on his hands, and fell asleep, his legs still in the water.

"Kaslin?"

He blinked awake. A weight sat on his stomach. He lifted his head enough to look, saw a purple-leaved plant anchored in his bellybutton, with brown roots trailing down across his stomach and between his legs. "What?" he said, stifling the urge to sit up and trying to remember where the plant had come from. He glanced up into a pale, hairless face. It took him a moment to recognize his mother without her eyebrows and her corona of dark hair.

"Are you all right?" she asked.

"I don't know. Are you?"

She blushed. "I suppose there are more embarrassing first

contact situations, but I can't think of any. At least the natives seem friendly. In their own way."

"I didn't know they'd do that to you," Kas said. "I'm sorry."

"It's all right," said his mother.

"Where's Avari?"

"I don't know. He fought a lot longer than I did, and he deployed his augmentations in the end. I think he hurt one of them. They carted him off. One of the others sent me down the second chute to you, brought me over here. He had to practically carry me. How do you navigate across this damned floor? Couldn't tell if it was quicksand or ice. Either way, slippery! I took a nap while I waited for you to wake up." She brushed off her wrist, stared at her chrono. "Your father is probably worried. It's almost night again."

"My plants hatched." He cupped a hand under the plant on his belly and sat up. Its walking roots reached around like a belt and clung to his waist. The ones between his legs drew up, their tips wet. It had a new stalk growing straight out from its center, with a bulging, sheathed bud at the end. "Avoz! Are you going to flower? Get away from me before you do," he muttered to the plant. The stalk curled up, the tip of the bud aimed toward his face. He put his hand over it and pushed it down. It obligingly curled the other direction, tip pointed toward his genitals. "Oh, God." He cupped his hands around the bud.

"They don't shoot their hosts," his mother said. "They have a sophisticated system for cross-pollinating. If you get a job as a colony, you'll find that you're never shot by the same plant twice. Do you think that's the kind of job you want, Kas?"

"No! No way!"

"Oh, good. I have higher hopes for you, but I want you to be happy."

"So it won't shoot me, huh? You're teasing me?" he muttered to his last plant. The woodwind music had faded to a single flute, which huffed out a series of short notes. The plant retracted its walking roots and pulled out of his navel, lowered itself to the ground, its blind bud bobbing as it strode away. He felt strangely bereft. Didn't it like him anymore? His navel felt strange, deeper than it had been. Had the little plant rooted to him through that channel? Had it been sucking on his stomach? He didn't feel too hungry at the moment, so whatever it had taken from him wasn't essential. He put his hand on the back of his neck. No more seed pits there, but raised, smooth bumps. Maybe he had scars now. "Mom?"

She settled beside him, stuck her toes into the water. "I'm starving," she said.

"Buk buk buk." He scooped up some floor, touched his tongue to it. A sharp lemon tang, with sweet overtones. "Taste it." He lifted his hand to her mouth. She hesitated, then licked at the stuff as though it were a snow cone. One taste and she pulled his hand to her mouth and ate all the powder he held.

"Hey. You can make your own. Remember? I showed you. Say 'buk' to make it soft and 'blook' to make it hard, 'beck' to make it sticky and 'bink' to make it light up. 'Bsstu' makes the light fade. 'Bufu' makes it unsticky. There's a bunch more, but I don't know what they mean. We always say 'bootah' to each other, but I still don't know why."

"Buk buk buk," she murmured and plunged her hand into the ground beside her, scooped up powder, dipped her tongue into it. She made a face. "But this tastes different."

"It tastes different everywhere. If you find a taste you like, save some for later." He checked her clothes for pockets. She wore a thin beige garment of wicking material that covered her body but not her arms or legs or head, the kind of unitard you wore under a biosuit if you didn't want to drown in your own sweat. The biosuit had all the pockets. "Or not," he said.

"This tastes moldy." She scooted over and bukked at a new patch of ground, lifted a handful and tasted. "Licorice. Better." She worked her way around the pool, edging farther from him with every experimental sampling of the ground.

He glanced after his baby plant, but he couldn't see it, or any of the others, anymore. He rose. "Mom, I'm going to look for Histly and Avari."

She scarfed another handful of white powder and got to her feet. "Weird. Like tasting lotus blossoms. I'll come with you."

He burbled a string of blooks, hardening a path for them, following traces of earlier trails across the cavern floor. The aliens didn't leave tracks, but he and Histly had. There were remnants of his previous blook-path.

"Speaking of colonies," said his mother. She walked behind him, using his path.

"What?" he asked. "Blook."

"You raised a record crop of assassin plants in a shorter time than anyone has before. Maybe the alien interference with your body was to make you a better colony host."

Kaslin groaned.

"Plus it didn't seem to make you stupid, just hungry. If you do it again, would you let me monitor you while it happens? I want to sample all the body chemistry the plants do on you, and there's still a lot to explore about your first modifications. Hmm. I guess I can test myself now, too. Yeah. Good."

"I don't want to be a colony again. They all left. I don't know where they went or if they're okay. I hate that."

"Fascinating," said his mother.

Three aliens drifted up to join them midway through the cavern. One gripped his shoulder, used other hands to turn him gently so it could examine his back. The others gathered, murmuring. Tonguetips tapped the places where he had hosted plants, not true licks but tastes. Each moist touch soothed him; he felt a tension he hadn't known he was holding drain away.

"Avoz," whispered his mother.

"What?" he asked, drowsy, his head drooping forward as they licked it.

"Instant healing, or something stranger. All signs of colonization vanish."

One of the aliens stroked a fuzzy hand from the top of his head down his neck and along his spine. He drew in a breath and straightened. He turned to look up into alien faces. "Histly," he said.

All three of them burst into boos. One took his hand and pulled him forward, blooking as it went. His mother followed. He glanced over his shoulder at her and realized she looked almost as alien as the large furry creatures following her. His own feet, white against the white ground, were like strange ghosts at the ends of his dark green pantlegs.

"What did you do to Histly?" he asked the aliens. They laughed boos again, knocking echoes loose from strange directions. The floor here was smooth and untouched until he and his mother stepped on it. They left slight imprints on the surface hardened by muttered blooks; alien feet walked weightless across it.

They went down a tunnel that was barely taller than the aliens, barely wider than three people side by side. Trails of pink lightspots wandered over ceiling, walls, and floors. As they progressed, the light tinted yellow, then pale green, a color he associated with ghosts in storyvids.

"Freak!" Histly screamed as he rounded a curve in the tunnel.

5

HE STOPPED, battered by the force of her anger. His mother bumped into him from behind.

"Two freaks!" Histly yelled. "Yeah! Come on and see me trapped here like some damned insect on display! Gloat, you scummy flutchcoster! Real chummy with the spiders, aren't you?"

Only her head was clearly visible, sticking out from the wall; the rest of her was wrapped in layers of white. She looked pretty much like her old self, shaggy pink head hair still intact, her skin still tan where it wasn't flushed with anger.

"Laugh. I dare you," she said, her cheeks red. "Just try it. Know if you do that when I get out of here, you're dead meat. Stinking dead meat. I'll kill you nice and slow, though, so it hurts a long time before you die."

"Histly," he said.

"I'll piss on your corpse. I'll set lyrinx bleeders on your dead body to chew it up and spit out mush so your family will be too disgusted to look at you after you're dead."

"Histly, stop it," Kaslin said. His voice came out in the hopeless, flattened tone it always squashed down to when he talked to her. He wished some new kid would move to Chuudoku so she would switch her attentions elsewhere, but he wasn't sure it would help. She seemed pretty fixated on torturing him.

"Does she always talk to you like this?" his mother muttered.

"No. Not always. Mostly she jabs me with one of her poisons and gloats while I suffer."

"Why didn't you tell me?"

"I did."

"Did you?"

"I told Dad. He told me if I just stood there and took it, she'd get tired of me and move on."

"What?" She turned away. "I really will strangle that man sometime in the near future."

"Are you laughing yet, freak?" Histly yelled.

"Do you hear me laughing?" said Kaslin. One of the aliens shoved him, and he stumbled toward Histly, startled. He glanced back. They had gathered again, silently, a looming host, his mother short and pale and lost-looking in the midst of all those long, brown, many-jointed legs. The nearest alien lowered its face toward him, the three eyes glistening, the flower stalks around its face swiveling, aiming the openings different directions. Kaslin narrowed his eyes. The flowers reminded him of the flowers on the assassin vines. Would these shoot seeds, too? Were the aliens related to the plant babies he had grown and lost?

The alien gripped his shoulders and walked him closer to Histly. "Bootah," it said. The others crowded close behind them, ringing him into a smaller and smaller space that included the wall tomb Histly was in.

"I swear, I'll spit on you," she yelled, her voice hurting his ears because she was so close. "I'll spit on you now and kill you later."

"Spit away. It's not like there's anything I can do about this," he said. "Look at them. They want something. They're not giving me much choice."

She breathed loudly through her nose.

"I think I'm supposed to kiss you," he said. One of the aliens pushed his head toward hers.

"I'll spit in your mouth," she said, her voice smaller. The tendons in her neck stood out, and she was red with effort that didn't seem to be paying off; she was still stuck.

"Okay," he said. He jerked loose of the alien hold, leaned in, and pressed his mouth to hers.

He couldn't tell if she spat in his mouth. His own was full of saliva flavored with lemons and mint from the last bite of floor he'd eaten. There was a flow as his lips locked on hers, something with a different flavor, still mint but maybe spearmint instead of peppermint. He thought of their first kisses, her forcing her mouth hard against his again and again when he couldn't fight her, his own lips slack against her assault, how the bruises and cuts his own teeth had made in his soft inner mouth had throbbed until he got treatment from the autodoc at home—he had been too ashamed to go to the school infirmary after the paralysis wore off, even though it was mostly automated. He would have had to show the school nurse how he was hurt so she could authorize treatment, and she would have put it on his record.

He could hurt Histly now, mash her good, bump her nose with his skull so hard he broke it. She was trapped. Only she wasn't paralyzed. Her lips moved against his. She could bite him if she wanted. He tasted salt, opened his eyes, realized tears flowed down her cheeks and mixed with their kiss. She tilted her head a little, and her tonguetip slipped into his mouth, moved along the inside of his upper lip, sliding past his teeth. He flinched, wondering if she was sucking on his lips so she could bite them. Her tongue touched his, slid under it, lifted his, and then she was sucking, definitely, but not biting, sucking on his tongue as though she were starving and he were food. Her breath hitched and speeded through her nose. His hands rose, reached for her, hit the wall. He whispered, "Buk buk buk," but his voice was silent. His lips were shaped wrong to do more than press in flutters against hers in the course of this strange, involved kiss. Still, the hard wall softened as he pressed his hands into it. Around him, the aliens were murmuring for him.

He dug through the softening wall, reached for her, found the solid of her arms and shoulders and upper body. He slid his hands past her and pulled her loose of her cocoon into his embrace, full frontal contact, while she mined his mouth.

She found her feet; instead of falling limp in his arms, she firmed her stance, tall, arrogant, feet spread wide. Her hands grasped his elbows, lifted him so his face stayed even with hers. His feet left the ground.

He didn't notice right away. He was too involved in what was happening between them at face level. But then he felt her fingernails digging into his arms, and chill fear unfolded from the base of his spine to flare upward. He pulled away from her, gasping. She followed until he turned his head. "Hey," she said. "Come back here."

"Let go."

"What?"

He twisted, wrenched his arms, kicked out, though not at her. "Let go."

She dropped him. One of the aliens steadied him so that he didn't fall down. "What?" she said. "Suddenly you're too good for me?" She leaned over and stared into his face. Her eyes were iridescent green. "You'll never convince me of that again, not after that liplock."

All the things he wanted to say to her rose in his mind, but he didn't open his mouth. "I'm afraid of you," occurred to him, and, "You hate me! You torture me! I hate you!" and, "What happens when you remember all those threats you made? Are you going to make good on them? I don't want to be paralyzed, puking, asleep, or whatever else you've got." He kept his silence instead.

"I own you now," she whispered, her mouth close to his. "Quit playing hard to get." She tilted his chin, cupped his face, and dropped her mouth on his again. He kept his feet, gripped her upper arms. Her fingernails didn't enter into it, so he relaxed and kissed her.

A while later she came up for air. "Okay. That's better," she said, and glanced around. "Hey." They were still surrounded by aliens, quiet now. Kaslin looked behind him. He didn't see his mother. He hadn't thought about her since he found Histly, but it finally occurred to him to wonder where she was. He was glad she wasn't in sight.

"Where are my clothes?" Histly asked.

Kaslin faced forward and realized he was staring straight at her breasts, which were just the right height. How could he have missed them? They weren't overwhelming, but they were big enough against her muscular chest, with small, dark brown aureoles. Her nipples looked hard and erect.

Histly noticed his regard. She pried his right hand loose from her upper arm and pressed his palm against her breast, then studied the effect. "Why are you so pale?" she asked. "What happened to your hair? Hey, how'd I get out of the wall?"

He worked her breast with his hand. Enough pillow there for him to enjoy the grip. Her nipple hardened more, sliding back and forth across his palm as he kneaded her. She put her hand over his. He stopped moving. She grinned. "Shy?"

"Oh, yeah," he said.

She didn't release him, just held his hand against her, still smiling. She glanced around, then behind her at the slashes on the wall where a hole her size still dented it. "You dug me out," she said. "How'd you do that? I couldn't even move." She dipped her head again, sought his mouth, kissed him deep. "You taste seriously fabulous. I never would have thought. Kas, what happened to you?"

"I don't know. Still trying to figure it out. The aliens did something to me."

"Does it have anything to do with hormones? You look really strange now. If I were in my right mind, I'd never think about you like this, but I can't help it."

"They fucked up my blood chemistry and took off all my hair. I don't know if it'll grow back. I don't get the ghost look, either. Why do they keep shoving us together?"

She growled as she looked past him toward the aliens. "Whatever it is, it worked, okay? You look at anyone else, I'll scratch your eyes out. And that includes your little buddy Maya. You're mine, understand?"

"Histly—"

"It's not a negotiation, Kas. It's a done deal." She pressed his hand tighter to her breast, then let go. He gave one last squeeze and let his hand drop. "Don't worry too much," she said. "I'll take care of you. I mean that in several ways. Behave, and life will be sweet for you."

"You have no idea what sweet means to me."

"Oh, yeah? Do *you* know?"

He turned away, stared at the scraped and pitted wall, searched for an answer. Things had been rushing by so fast he hadn't had time to get used to any of the new stuff. What did he even want anymore?

Figuring out how things worked in here excited him. Finding out about the tastes in the walls, too—testing them, choosing the ones he liked best, eating as much as he wanted. He and his parents had lived on a limited food budget back on Hitherto. Since moving to Chuudoku, the food restrictions had eased, but he never felt like he could eat as much as he wanted of anything.

As a plant parent, that had been his mandate. He almost hadn't been able to keep up with the demand. He had liked doing that: something he was good at.

The aliens hadn't tried to slow him down when he sampled the walls and floors. Eating. One of his favorite new pleasures.

He poked a finger at the softened wall, tasted the tip. Vanilla ice cream, orange syrup. He filled a pocket.

"What are you doing?" Histly asked as though she were more interested than annoyed.

"It's food."

"Is that what makes your mouth taste so great?" She scooped

out some wall, touched the tip of her tongue to it. "Yuck!" She spat, flung the powder away. He touched the place she had scooped from, tasted it. Chocolate cake. He filled another pocket.

"How can you eat that?"

"What does it taste like to you?"

"Sand that sucks my mouth dry. Powdered glass."

"Chocolate cake."

"Really?"

He bit into a handful and nodded.

"Show me." She gripped his head and kissed him, moaned as her tongue tangled with his. He still had powder in his mouth; she licked and sucked it into her mouth, moaning and shuddering, till she cleaned him out. "Oh, God, Kas. You're an interface. Make me some more. That's the best chocolate cake I've ever had, and I'm sooo hungry."

Too weird, if she could only taste it after he did. It reminded him of the feeding habits of baby birds, who ate things their parents had already eaten and regurgitated. He filled his mouth with powder, waited until the thick chocolate taste was solid on his tongue, then pulled her down and pressed his lips to hers.

Her hands closed and opened convulsively on his shoulders as she cleaned out his mouth.

What if he said no to her? Would she hurt him?

He hadn't wanted to say no. This strange exchange heated him in surprising ways. It wasn't just that he was going to cream his pants, though one more moan from her—okay, that was it, without even priming the pump. He was gone.

"Damn," she muttered a little later, when she'd licked every trace of powder off his tongue. "What a waste. Why didn't you say something? I want you inside me."

"You *do?*"

"What part of 'I own you' don't you understand?" She slid a hand inside the waistband of his pants, massaged the stik-tites and tugged them open. "God. You're the same all over. Yesterday I would have called you a maggot. How come I think you're candy now?" She explored and fondled him, then tucked him back into his pants and wiped her hand off on his butt. His hands were clenched so tight they ached. "Tell me when you're ready again. Speaking of ready—more cake."

"Just a sec." He packed two pockets from the place with the cake taste, then went back to the vanilla-and-orange site and stuffed his mouth with it. He worked it with his tongue, then went to her and tugged her down.

She tasted, broke away. "What?" She returned, sucked eagerly. "How did you do that?"

"It's different everywhere."

"That's spooky." She glanced wildly around, gripped his hand. Most of the aliens had faded. "This? This hard-soft stuff is—" She shook her head. "Daddy's going to plutch when he finds out what's down here."

"Do you have to tell him?"

"Do I have to— Kas." She took a big breath, let it out. "You're new here. But how dumb can you really be?" She kissed the top of his head. "Doesn't matter. You're mine. The discoveries here? The pharmacological potentials? The new kind of alien, no matter how creepy they are? Whoever controls these resources can move up so high in the gov. A mansion on Rimini is just a start."

"You really think you can control the aliens?"

"Once we find the right lever, sure," she said. "The xenososhes will have to get on it, but Chuudoku has the best."

"Who's in charge at the moment?"

"Give me a little more of that ice cream stuff, will you? I'm almost full, Kas. Sure feels good after all the growling my stomach did."

He sighed and worked up another mouthful for her. Her feeding wasn't as frenzied this time; she was more relaxed, almost tender. Afterward, she rubbed her cheek on his and said, "Thanks. Kas, can you get us out of here?"

"Probably."

She rubbed off her wrist chrono. "We've been down here a whole day. God, it feels like a lot longer. I spent so much time in that stupid pit, and then they showed up, the scutching spiders, and they stole my clothes and licked me and—Avoz, they know me better than my doctor! They paralyzed my arms and dragged me around for a while, and eventually they locked me in the wall." She flexed her fingers, frowned at her hands. "I couldn't move anything but my head," she said. "But now they're—" She flicked her left index finger, and the augmented nail shot out from beneath her regular nail. It was tinted blue. "I wonder," she said, looking sideways at him.

"No." Which nail was it? He'd never seen her using them. By the time he knew she had jabbed him with them, it was too late.

She curled her finger and the nail sank out of sight. "Maybe later. When we're out of here."

"No. No more, Histly. Make jokes about wanting me and owning me, okay. Cute. But I'm not going to stand still for any more of that poison stuff."

"How you gonna stop me?"

He took three steps away from her, feeling a strange hot squeeze in his chest, a sour taste across his tongue. He had liked liking her. He had hoped it meant they were on a different footing from their earlier relationship.

"Seriously," she said. "How?"

"Bike," he whispered, and the ground rose up and wrapped around her.

"Good one," she said, her voice muffled through layers of floor. She cut her way free in seconds. Her hands looked different, fingers and palms flat, the edges along her pinkies hard and sharp. She shook her hands and they shifted back to normal. "Stuff I said before? No joke, Kas. You are *so* mine."

He shook his head. "Not if you poison me."

"All right. I used to love watching you squirm, but it's not as fun anymore. No poison."

He relaxed, then wondered if her word was good. Why should it be?

"It's sexy you can make this white stuff do tricks, the way they can." She came to him, kissed him quickly. "What else can you make it do?"

He smiled a little and shook his head. "Anyway, when we get out, you won't want me anymore. I look even worse in daylight."

"You've already been out?"

"Yeah."

"You came back. You brought someone? You brought help, Kas?"

"Sort of."

She hugged him. "I didn't think you were ever coming back," she whispered. She shoved him away.

He didn't fall this time. He took two steps back and stood, his feet dug into the ground. "You gave me so many reasons to rescue you, didn't you?"

She rubbed her eyes. "Sorry. Yeah, you're right. I shouldn't blame you for not wanting to come back. I—" She hugged him again. "Thanks."

"Okay," he said.

"I want you now, and I'll want you later."

"You won't. People will make fun of you. I do look like a maggot."

"People won't make fun of me," she said.

"You can't beat up everybody, Histly. There are people with better augmentations than yours."

"Maybe. But you, Kas, nobody else has you. You're the best augmentation ever."

"What do you mean?"

"Never mind. Which way is out?"

He paused, got his bearings. Some of the aliens were near, but not very near, lurking shadows down the tunnel or behind them.

The place in the wall where Histly had been made a good landmark. Travel away from it. The tunnel led only one direction from here. The light was greenish at this end; the floor was still hard enough to support them. He took her hand and led her out.

"How come this floor is hard and it was soft where I fell in?"

"It's variable," he said.

"How do you know where it's safe to walk?"

"I'm following our footprints in." The scuff marks of his and his mother's footprints were very faint, but they still cast slender shadows, even in the diffuse pink light.

"Oh," said Histly. "I see now. Who came in with you?"

"Mom."

"You brought your mother? That other maggot was your mother? The aliens augmented her, too? Where is she now?"

"I don't know. I think she went to find her partner. We lost him on the way in."

"Why'd you bring your mother?"

"She's a med tech. Histly, you know you have a locator?"

"Sure. Every kid gets an implant when they're born, and we have regular updates every couple years. Oh, shit."

"Oh, shit?"

Histly checked her chrono. "Hmm. They might not be looking for me yet. I make myself obnoxious so nobody looks for me right away. Gives me more freedom." She tapped a hotspot on her chrono and pressed its face into her other shoulder, then lowered it. "Nobody's tripped it in the past day, but the sooner we get out of here, the better. Ma never lets me stay away longer than about a day without checking on me. They'll be able to backtrack if they get curious, so I better not make them curious. Can you speed it up a little?"

"Sure." He ran along their backtrail, and she followed. He had a flash of déjà vu, the many times she'd chased him. He glanced back, saw her ferocious smile, figured she was remembering, too. She ran so easily. She could pass him any time she wanted; now that he'd shown her how to find the trail, he wondered why she didn't.

"Is that water?" she asked as they ran to the lake where he had submerged himself when he was still raising the plants. She threw herself down on her stomach and lowered her face to the lake, drank deep. He dropped beside her, lifted water in his hand and drank. Then he tested the scuffed up places along the shore where his mother had tried her first alien food, found some tastes he liked, and finished stuffing the rest of his cargo pockets. He wasn't sure when he'd get back.

"Slip me some of that," Histly said as he closed the last stik-tite on one of his thigh pockets. He filled his mouth with pomegranate pineapple, waited until he had worked it around, then tilted up his head and let her drink from him. Her lips rested against his even after she'd taken everything he had. Her arms had wrapped around him. She turned half away and laughed, her breath huffing past his cheek. "I had no idea I could have so much fun without hurting somebody," she said. She rose, carrying him with her. "That didn't hurt, did it?"

"Nope."

She set him on his feet and dusted off the back of his pants, pinched his butt, but not hard enough to hurt, just enough to surprise him. "I want to come back here with you and try lots more things, but first I have to establish a regular outside presence. Ready?"

"Yep." He took off again, and she followed so close he imagined he could feel her stepping on his shadow. They passed the thrashed-out pit where he had first left her. Presently they came to the base of the first slope. He stopped and looked up.

"Slippery. I remember falling down that thing. How'd you get up there last time?" she asked.

"One of the aliens carried me."

She stooped, her back to him. "Climb on, Kas. I've got climbing augs in my hands and feet."

Stranger things, he supposed, had happened, even in the past hour. He climbed on her back, wrapped his legs around her waist. He slipped his arms under hers and reached up to grip her shoulders from the front. She tapped one heel into the side of her other foot. A piton tip shot out from under her toes, a sharpened steel spike. She repeated the action with her other foot. She fitted her hands together at the places where her thumbs met her index fingers and pressed, and the fingers of both hands melted into hardened wedges. "Hang on," she said, and plunged hands and feet into the white slope.

She picked her way up. Every once in a while she'd stop. "How about here?" She'd offer him powder from the slope in front of her on the plate of her hand, and he would taste it. If it tasted good, he hauled himself forward to meet her mouth and feed her some. She loved the fiery mouthful of chiles, but she spat out the lavender pastille.

They reached the first plateau and stopped. "Any water here?" she asked.

"I never saw any." He glanced around. They had lost their alien escort. What was that about? Now that they had forced him and Histly together, their work was done? What kind of weird matchmakers were they?

He wanted to bink the lights so he could see farther, but he didn't want Histly to know he could do that. "The second slope is shorter, and the school isn't that far away. We can get water at the fountain."

"All right. Come on."

She picked her way up the second slope even more quickly, unhitched him from her back, clicked away her augmentations, and turned back into a spectacular naked woman. The harsh light of outside hurt his eyes again, even though it was almost evening. He blinked into normal sight and followed her out into the upper air.

"Well, this is a little obvious," Histly said as they headed toward the school. She fingered a wound in a tree where Avari had shot off a spike to let them through, then pointed to another wound on the next tree.

"We were in a hurry."

"You and the two med techs you brought to save me?"

He walked past her. "I had more than one reason for coming back, Histly. While I was out here trying to hide, I got colonized by assassin plants."

"What?" She gripped his shoulders, pulled him to a stop, studied his back. "What? They didn't even leave traces. Did you pull them out and survive?" She checked her chrono. "How'd you get rid of them so fast?"

"So my mom's a med tech and she wanted to study me, and so did her partner, but first they had to figure out how to feed me and my colony. The new body is a perfect substrate for growing assassin plants from larvae to nymphs overnight. The powder is the perfect food."

"Overnight," she repeated. She pressed points in his back, shook her head, and let him go. "There are two med techs running around down in our cavern, unsupervised."

"And thirty-three new assassin plant nymphs scattered all over."

"Thirty-three? Avoz! We have to get down to the property office and buy this place before anybody else finds out anything."

"What?" Kaslin said.

"This is the biggest discovery on Chuudoku in a long time, Kas. There are so many business and social repercussions. You might not recognize the huge potential here unless you studied revolutionary information systems. Kind of my favorite subject."

"Huh," he said. "Okay. If you say so. Listen, Histly. I can't go home. Soon as any legitimate scientists see me, they're going to lock me up and make me disappear. I'll get you to school, but after that, I'm going to hide out in the forest, okay?"

"No."

"What do you mean?"

"You're not taking me seriously, Kas. I wish you'd take me seriously. You're mine. I won't let any scientists lock you up and study you except mine."

"I don't want to be locked up."

"Just for a little while. I won't let them dissect you or make you disappear. Okay?"

"No!"

"Just agree with me. We don't have to fight about this."

"Just because you say you own me doesn't make it true."

She grabbed him and kissed him and smiled at him. "You are so cute, in a totally maggoty way. I knew there was some reason I kept chasing you, even before all the modifications."

"Histly—"

They emerged from the spike tree grove into the parking lot. Histly froze, and Kaslin stalled beside her. The ambulance that had brought him and his mother and Avari here was parked in front of the school, next to Histly's purple UltraScoot. Beside her vehicle, there was a top-of-the-line red and silver skimmer, its driver-side door open. A tall, ostentatiously augmented man in expensive clothes leaned against the skimmer, his arms crossed over his chest. He smiled at them.

"Well, Histly. What have you done this time?" he asked. His voice was rich and ominous.

"Hi, Daddy. I'll cut you in if you take us to the property office right away."

He stepped away from the car. "You can make a buy from the car console."

She nodded and pushed past him, dropped into the driver's seat, and pushed sensidots to call up a screen. A headset dangled from the ceiling, and she slipped it on. Bewildered, Kaslin watched from the sidelines. Histly tapped sensidots, spoke softly into the headset's mike. She touched another control on the console and a hidden storage compartment opened. She took out two water bulbs, drank from one, handed him the other, distracted. He drank.

"Where'd she lose her clothes?" Histly's father asked Kaslin after Kaslin had finished the water, which didn't taste as good as the water in the cavern.

"I'm not exactly sure," Kaslin said in the same squashed, toneless voice he used to use to talk to Histly. There was something about this guy that made Kaslin fear him, a combined bulldozer/pull-the-arms-off-small-children aura.

"Did you tear them off her?"

Since he'd been thinking about removing arms, it took Kaslin a moment to realize the man was still talking about Histly's clothes. "No, sir."

"What kind of mutant freak are you?"

"Daddy, quit teasing Kaslin and let me concentrate."

"Kaslin," muttered the man. His eyes unfocused and the eyeballs darted from side to side. He must have eye screens, expensive implants that responded to eye movements. Subtle users could scan information without the person they were talking to even being aware the other was consulting outside sources, but

Histly's dad had no reason to be subtle with Kaslin. When the man smiled, he showed augmented teeth, sharp canines in his lower jaw that pushed points into his upper lip. Kaslin figured it was a calculated business move.

"Ha," said Histly. "No more legal, upper division ed, or new augs funds left, but I'm owner of record now. Dad, you're in for thirty percent. I had to use the whole discretionary fund at the business."

"This better be good, Kitten."

She shrugged out of the headset and console, brushed across the return buttons so all the extra equipment disappeared, and climbed out of the car. "Even I don't know how good yet." She stretched, then put her hands on Kaslin's shoulders from behind. "Say hi to the ambassador to a brand new sentient race here on Chuudoku."

Her father's eyebrows twitched. "Hello, Ambassador."

Kaslin lifted a hand and twiddled his fingers in an abbreviated wave, then glared over his shoulder at Histly.

She came around in front of him and patted his cheek. "I bought your first six years of work rights, too, Kas. Your dad's so deep in debt already he sold you cheap. Be nice to me, or it's going to be six years of solid assassin-plant colonization, one brood after another."

"You wouldn't."

"Come on, Kas. How well do we know each other? You ought to know by now that I rarely resist dares."

"Okay. Sorry. It's not a dare. What do you want, Histly?"

She glanced at her father, flickered her eyelids, turned and focused on Kaslin's face. "Maximum financial opportunity," she said. The tip of her tongue touched her upper lip as she faced him, away from her father, and he realized that she was hiding, too, already hiding in plain sight, somehow. He wasn't sure what she was hiding, or what she really meant by any of it. "I can use your help. Cooperate, and the benefits will be so big I'll cut you in for a few of them just to be nice. Resist and—you know how I am about things like that, Kas."

He decided he'd be better off not answering her.

"Is the ambassador coming home with us, Histly?" said her father.

"Of course," said Histly.

Kaslin looked toward the forest. "Mom," he said.

"Don't you think she's safe?" Her tone was gentle for the first time since they had come face to face with her father.

He thought about that. Safer with the aliens than at home, though he couldn't be sure about Avari. No way to tell what was happening with Avari.

"I'll take you back tomorrow, after we make sure we have all the legal stuff covered. Get in." Histly opened the back door of the red and silver skimmer, held it. He slid in and across the seat to the far side. Histly ducked her head to follow.

"Hold it," said her father. He went around to the back of the car and popped the storage space, pulled out a blue blanket. "I'm not driving through town with my daughter naked in the back seat, no matter how comfortable you are in your skin."

"Oh, Daddy," she said. She wrapped the blanket around her, pressed stiktites at the edges to make an improvised dress out of it. She slid into the skimmer and belted in, then reached across the seat for Kas's hand. His first impulse was to draw away from her, but he ditched that impulse and gripped her fingers. If she was going to poison him, no time like the present.

If everything she said was true, she had the legal right to do it anytime she liked.

She didn't poison him. Instead she fell asleep, slumped closer and closer to him until her head rested on his shoulder; her breath brushed his neck as it eased in and out. Kaslin watched streets and suburbs of Ash flash by below as they wove farther into the cityweb. The skimmer pulled into a port on the top story of the tallest building downtown. The doors popped open. Histly's father got out and opened the door on Kaslin's side of the car. He glared. "Do you want to carry my daughter inside, or should I do it?" he asked, in that warm, rich, scary voice.

Kaslin licked his lips, leaned forward, and kissed Histly. She responded avidly, then opened her eyes. "What?"

"We're home."

"Huh? Oh." She stretched, yawned against the back of her hand, and climbed out of the car. "Come on. I'll introduce you to everybody."

Kaslin slid out of the car. His bare feet sank into floor fleece. They carpeted their carport? He closed his eyes and worked his toes into the fleece, which embraced his feet.

Histly laughed. "This is just the allweather stuff. Come inside. It's nicer there. Though, now that you don't mention it—" She slid around on the floor fleece, too, her toes flexing.

"Histly. Your mother's waiting," her father said, and went inside.

She took Kaslin's arm and tugged him through the portal into the penthouse. On the threshold, he felt a shock go through him, but Histly pulled him across, and it faded. She was right, the floor fleece here was luxurious. Nanos in it cleaned all the dirt off his feet; he felt it as a faint sizzle.

The room they entered was an antechamber. The floor fleece was many colors of pink, streaked with gold. Art arrangements stood in informal groups around the edges of the room: collections of intentional sticks dipped in metallic colors; a three-dee collage that shifted in the air, constantly reforming its parts into different wholes; a many-leveled planter with a different kind of pine bonsai at each level; a small fountain whose water flowed across a tilted rock wall. The air was scented like some wild outdoors Kaslin had never been to, only seen in vids. It was a strange sensation, smelling something he'd only imagined smelling.

"My love," Histly's father said. Kaslin turned, realized that something he'd mistaken for peripheral sculpture was actually a human. An angular, black-haired woman in a scarlet and white robe turned toward the man, who said, "Come see what Histly's brought home this time."

The woman glided toward him. She laughed, a glass wind-chime sound. "Is it be-kind-to-the-handicapped week?" she asked, and touched the top of Kaslin's head with two fingertips. The needle slid under his skin so smoothly it didn't hurt at all. The poison worked instantly; he lost voluntary muscle control and slumped to the floor, sprawled in a graceless heap. He couldn't even blink.

"Mother!" Histly yelled.

"Panda," said Histly's mother. "Put this in the closet for now."

Peripherally Kaslin saw a large dark shape dart out of an alcove. Then he saw it directly as it bent over him. It looked like an actual bear of some kind, though not a panda; it was glossy black, with white spectacle marks on its chest. It squatted beside him and pushed its paws under him, lifted him like a coat lying across its forearms, and shuffled toward one of the doorways. Kaslin's head flopped back. He stared at a sculpture he hadn't noticed before: a spinning mobile of small, feather- less birds, naked in their pink skins, beaks open, but whether to scream or sing he couldn't tell.

"Mother!" Histly screamed. "How could you?"

The top of Kaslin's head warmed, then burned. He lifted a hand and rubbed it. The burn faded.

The bear paused, peered down at him, confused. Kaslin pulled himself together and rolled off its outstretched arms, almost managing to land on his feet, but not quite. "You peo- ple," he said.

Histly's mother stared at him, her eyes so wide the whites showed all around her irises. Her startled face was momentary; she clicked back into distant and untouched, possibly amused or offended.

Histly raced to Kaslin and jerked him to his feet. "You don't," she said, "treat my ambassador to a local sentient alien race like my boyfriends." Then, softer, "You okay?"

"Score one for fucked-up body chemistry," he muttered.

"Panda, return," Histly's mother said. The bear lumbered back to its alcove.

Histly took Kaslin's hand and led him to where her parents were standing. "This is Kaslin Davorna, who just discovered that Chuudoku has an indigenous, intelligent race in a cavern on land that Daddy and I just bought, along with mining and exploitation rights for everything on or under it. Kaslin and I both made first contact with the aliens, but he was much more successful. Kaslin, these are my parents, Peck and Lilia Mapworth."

Neither of them offered their hands.

"Miz and Mr. Mapworth," Kaslin said, and tilted his head while his brain clicked into high gear. Mapworth was the head of the trade commission, one of the highest officials on the planet. Miz Mapworth was the daughter of the president-for-life. Kaslin was sure Histly had a different last name. Histly Etasha. His insides curdled. Maybe he should have let the bear put him in the closet.

"Davorna," said Mr. Mapworth.

"Sir," said Kaslin.

"Welcome to the penthouse, boy. Are you hungry?"

The question was more complicated than Kaslin expected. He'd had a lot of food in his mouth recently, but fed most of it to Histly. What answer did Mr. Mapworth want? "I suppose I am."

"Supper," Mr. Mapworth said.

Kaslin glanced at Histly, wondering if an answer was called for. She slid her arm through his and led him toward another door. The Mapworths followed, but paused a short distance away to confer in low voices.

As he and Histly approached, the door lifted, revealing a mushroom dining table and a surround of short-backed stools on a green fleece carpet. Most of the walls in this room had livetime Paradise forest scenes from floor to ceiling; one wall was an active but quiet fountain. The ceiling had livetime sky on it, evening colors now; low lights inset in the table made it glow a soft gold. The room even had a faint forest smell, fresh green plants and soft flowery scents, unlike any of the forests on Chuudoku, which tended to smell acrid or rank or just strange.

As they crossed the threshold, Kaslin felt a simmering shock from head to toes. He looked up. The threshold was wider than most. It must include a scanner; he'd never felt one like that before. He glanced at Histly.

"I forgot," she said. "You're totally recorded into the house system now."

"Totally?"

Her mouth dropped open, then firmed into a frown. "Damn. I forgot you're so maggoty inside and out. I'm getting used to you. Yes, a medscan's included. Business advantage for Daddy to know if his associates have physical problems. Most people can't tell they've been scanned. But you could?"

"Kind of a jolt."

"You get more interesting all the time." She tugged his arm and they moved on to the table. Her parents crossed the threshold after them. Ms. Mapworth was not looking at her husband. Mr. Mapworth stared at Histly, then got that unfocused look that indicated he was watching information scroll across his eye screens. His eyebrows rose.

"Fidi," said Ms. Mapworth. "It's suppertime, and we have company."

"Coming," said a high, young voice out of the air.

Ms. Mapworth advanced to the table and waved her hand over the command pad. Sensidots rose, and she programmed a meal and dishes. Mr. Mapworth went to a niche cleverly disguised as a hole in one of the livetime forest tree trunks. He tapped a pillowbug, and the hole widened to reveal a bar set. "What would you like to drink, Davorna?"

"Water, please," Kaslin said.

"Me, too, Daddy. Lots," said Histly.

Mr. Mapworth turned; he held a tray with five tall blue glasses on it. He brought it to the table. "Please. Take seats," he said, gesturing to stools on either side of the one he stood behind.

Kaslin exchanged glances with Histly. He wished he knew her better so they had had time to develop a dictionary of signals. Then he thought how odd that wish was, considering where they had been in their relationship two days ago. She jerked her head toward her father's left, and went to her father's right. Kaslin went to the left-hand stool and stood behind it as Mr. Mapworth set drinks at five places. He wished they had stopped somewhere on the way to the penthouse so he could have picked up some clothes. A shirt, at least, to cover the blinding whiteness of his hairless chest, the too-soft pink of his nipples now; shoes might also have helped. His pants were ragged, powdered with cavern dust, stained by plant and liquid encounters, and torn from various chases he'd been through. Indestructible, ha! So much for catalog copy.

"*Ewww!*" said a voice.

6

Kaslin glanced up, met Fidi's horrified stare. She stood on the threshold of a different door, another section of livetime tree trunk that had slid up and open. Fidi, Histly's younger sister, was clothed in something that was shades of pale, scarfy purple, tight on her upper body above the waist, billowy and skirted below. Her hair was as riotous and red as always, a crinkling gingery halo around her head. The colors of her hair and her dress clashed. Still, she looked like a fairy emerging from a hollow tree.

"What are you?" she whispered.

"Fidi," he said.

She took three steps toward him. "Kaslin?" Then she raced up and touched his cheek. She frowned, a pucker between her brows. "You're—bleached? Bald? What happened to you?"

He shook his head and smiled at her. "Nobody knows yet."

"Fidi? You know Davorna?" asked Mr. Mapworth.

"Sure. He's in my game club."

"What?" Histly said, in her old, mean voice. She stared past her father at Kaslin, her eyes narrow.

"One way to get away from you was to join an extracurricular activity," he said. "Gaming's a natural for me. I spent a lot of my life before Chuudoku in refugee camps. Nothing else to do."

"So that's where you went," Histly said. Her smile was a sneer. "It's not going to work again."

"Nothing's going to work the way it used to." Kaslin sighed and pulled out his stool. He had been waiting for the others to sit down before he did, but suddenly he felt tired. If they were going to be rude and stay standing all this time, he decided he could be rude, too, and maybe collapse.

"Have you made a habit of pursuing this boy?" Ms. Mapworth said.

"She's been obsessed with him for three months," said Mr. Mapworth. "Ever since he arrived on the planet."

Histly stared at her father.

"Come now," he said. "I'm interested in everything you do, Histly."

Fidi went to the stool to Kaslin's left and sat down on it. She toed a control and the stool scooted up to the table. "She's the favorite," Fidi whispered, not very quietly, to Kaslin.

"I get that," Kaslin whispered back.

Ms. Mapworth told the table it was time to serve. She took a place on the far side of Histly, and spoke words in a different language to make her appliances behave. The meal spots sank under the surface, replaced with place settings replete with plates full of delicious-smelling and -appearing food: roast cline, gravy, potatoes, menument salads, fruit carved and mosaicked into the shape of rabbits.

"Please," said Ms. Mapworth. "Sit. Enjoy."

Kaslin waited until Fidi took the first bite. He wasn't sure what the utensils were for; there were six of them around his plate, three of which he'd never seen before. Fidi ate slowly. He mimed her. None of the food tasted good; he only ate a little.

"Now you'll explain to me what the ambassador title means, Histly," Ms. Mapworth said when most people had finished enough food. "Why should we respect this boy more than your standard obsessions?"

Histly set down her knife and turned away from the table. "Clear," she said. The walls went blank, except for doorways, panels, and niches Kaslin could see, now that the forest wasn't rustling and breezing and obscuring them. Histly tapped her temple just above her eye. Light shone from her pupil, spread against the wall, showed a dim image: a fuzzy representation of one of the aliens, lumbering and furry, the face a caricature, the limbs many and shifting. "That's alive down in the cavern," she said.

"So what? Just another variant of the lerts," said Mr. Mapworth.

Histly blinked and the image shifted. More aliens, and Kaslin among them, looking back and forth, his mouth moving. They towered over him. Ms. Mapworth gasped.

"Oh, God," muttered Mr. Mapworth.

It looked like Kaslin was arguing with them. One nudged him. Another gave his shoulder a push. Then he was falling forward toward the viewpoint, eclipsing everything else in the image. Histly closed her eyes. The projection stopped.

"You're wired?" Kaslin said.

"Duh."

He was glad she'd stopped projecting before he had started kissing her, which he thought was what had happened next.

"Are they as big as they look?" asked Mr. Mapworth.

"Do they really have faces?" Fidi asked.

"Faces, tools, culture, weird white stuff that changes according to their desires."

"What?"

"Kas. Unpack me some of that chocolate cake, will you?"

He wanted to resist. He had shared this with Histly, but he didn't want to share it with her parents. They were giant predators, and all he'd learned to be was prey.

He had only Histly's word that she'd bought his work rights. But why would she lie about a thing like that? If she actually owned his work rights, he was bound to her and had to obey any orders she gave him so long as they didn't pose a danger to himself. There were loopholes around the danger-to-himself clause, too. Legally, she could do all kinds of nasty things to him, and he had no recourse. If he disobeyed her, she had a lot of measures she could pursue to make him behave, and in any dispute, the police would help her, not him.

He dug a handful of white flakes out of a cargo pocket. He couldn't remember if it was the cake. He set them carefully on the placemat on the table.

"Chocolate cake," said Ms. Mapworth.

"Taste it."

"I'm not going to eat something that's never been tested, Histly!"

She rose from her chair, came around to stand behind Kas. "We're going to need to do extensive testing on this stuff, Ma, Dad. It's everything to the aliens. Food, building material, light source. I don't know how much it can do, but I bet Kas does." Histly licked her finger and stuck it in the white powder, touched powder to her tongue, made a face. "When I eat it, it tastes like sawdust. Kas puts it in his mouth—" She lifted a fingerful, slid it past his lips onto his tongue. He drew in a deep breath. The powder tasted so much better than dinner had. His true food, he was afraid, from now on. It was the chocolate cake after all. He crushed it between his tongue and the roof of his mouth, and the flavor burst through him.

Histly kissed him, and he offloaded some of the chocolate onto her tongue. She gasped and licked, took it all.

A crack sounded. Histly startled up and away. At first Kaslin was angry that he had lost the connection, and then he remembered where he was and was angry Histly had initiated it. He blinked. Ms. Mapworth's plate lay broken in front of her.

"We aren't here to watch you enter into an orgy," she said.

Histly gripped Kaslin's head near the base of his skull. "It's not an orgy, Ma. I'm sorry, I guess that wasn't the best demonstration. To me, this white stuff tastes like sawdust. Kas puts it in his mouth, and I take it from him, and then it's chocolate cake, or lemon juice, or filufa fruit, or some other flavor. Once he's tasted it, I can taste it, too. They changed him so he can process their food and make it palatable to us. Daddy, you get it, don't you? Kas is half-alien already. He's a factory, in more ways than one. There's an assassin plant application, too."

Fidi jumped up. "Kas, can I try that?" she asked.

"No!"

Fidi turned to her sister. "Histly?"

Histly frowned at Fidi, then reached for the powder. She scooped some up. "Come on, babe." She tugged down on his chin, and he let her open his mouth. This was too weird, everything about it was weird and strange; what if her parents decided they didn't want Histly messing around with him this way? They could have him cut up for parts. They could make a drum kit out of his skin, and be within their legal rights. She pressed powder to his tongue. He worked it into a tasty paste.

"Go on," she said to Fidi, who leaned forward—that faint flower smell he had noticed about her, Fidi, the augmented sister, two years younger, who had never bullied him, who had taught him a couple of new games. They were well-matched and often played together. She could beat him, but only half the time. She was good-natured and friendly. He had never been able to believe she was related to Histly.

She kissed him, tentatively, as though she'd never tried anything like that before. Performance, he knew. She had a boyfriend named Jorge, and Kaslin had seen them kissing passionately under the stairs at school. Fidi kissed him, and he opened his mouth and pushed some of the chocolate paste into hers. She moaned with delight and licked it off his tongue until Mr. Mapworth dragged her up and away from him. Fidi gave a little cry, then pressed her hand to her mouth.

Kaslin swallowed, shook his head. He glared at Histly.

Mr. Mapworth handed him a spoon. "Does it work without the physical contact?"

"Good idea," said Histly. "One more time, Kas. When it's ready, spit it on the spoon."

He didn't want to. He hated that Histly thought of him as a factory. Had she been thinking that all along?

What had he really expected from his life? Being a refugee meant being shuffled around at other people's whims, because other people had done something wrong. He hated his father. When they got to Chuudoku, aside from his bully problems with Histly, Kaslin had thought things might be different. He was getting the same education other kids got. Some of them were on track to be colonies for assassin plants or something worse, some to be trials, and some to be in charge of things. His mother had him half convinced he could do something besides be soil for plants or a guinea pig for new drug trials. She had started a savings account for a career module for him. If he showed any definite aptitudes, the gov would donate half the module; they cultivated useful citizens. He hadn't figured out what he wanted most to do yet, aside from alien contact, but possibilities had opened up.

Now, factory *and* colony. Yay.

He took some of the powder from the table and put it in his mouth, worked it with his tongue until the taste was all through it again, and stuck the spoon in his mouth. He scooped up some of the chocolate and swallowed the rest. He handed the spoon to Histly. She thought she was his master. If he acted as though he believed it, maybe, sooner or later, she would lower her guard.

She handed the loaded spoon to her father, who frowned at the white paste, then scanned it with a small device, plugged the device into a port below his wrist chrono, and watched readouts on his eye screens. After a moment he tasted the powder. His eyebrows peaked again. He handed the half-full spoon to Ms. Mapworth, who touched the tip of her tongue to it, meditated for a few seconds, then took another lick.

Kaslin crossed his arms, feeling grumpy. Was performing animal better than colony or factory?

"How does this make you an ambassador?" Fidi asked him.

"It has nothing to do with being an ambassador. Histly's

making it all up. The aliens didn't entomb me in a wall the way they did her, but we weren't exactly communicating, either."

"Entomb Histly in a wall?" said Fidi.

"You were doing something right," Histly said. "At least you were loose. You were leading them around, and they were leading you around. You weren't restrained the way I was."

"How were you restrained?" Mr. Mapworth asked.

"They seemed mad at me from the start. First they checked me out in all possible ways I can think of—Dad, there may be trauma involved, so I hope you have a good counseling program. There might even be medical complications."

"Your scan shows that you're in perfect health," said Mr. Mapworth. "Your mental scan shows no abnormalities."

"Oh, good." She sounded disappointed. "So these giant spiders totally groped me, and then they trussed me up. I was underground for nearly twenty-six hours, and I spent most of it in a pit, or trussed up by a bunch of spiders, or trapped in a wall. I need better social skills."

"How'd you get out of the wall?"

"Kaslin dug me out. The wall was made out of this stuff." She picked up a pinch of white powder. "It all looks like this down there, but sometimes it's hard, sometimes it's soft, it all tastes different, and sometimes it lights up. The cavern is full of this stuff, Daddy."

"The wall was so hard you couldn't free yourself, and Ambassador Boy dug you out?"

"How'd you do that, Kas?" Histly asked, curious. "My augmentations didn't work. What did you do?"

"People have been jerking me around a lot lately," Kaslin said. "I don't like it. I know you people can squash me flat, but somehow that doesn't make me feel like telling you anything. All I have is information. If you offer me something in exchange, I might be inclined to give it to you."

"Or I could torture it out of you, always fun for me," said Histly.

"True." He shrugged. "Maybe what you get from me that way won't be as accurate. And, because I have altered body chemistry, your usual techniques might not work the way you think they will."

"What do you want, Kas?" Fidi asked.

"A shower. Some clothes. A little dignity, maybe. Asking instead of telling. Legal emancipation from my father before he drags me even deeper into his debt structure. Time to rescue my mom and her partner from the cavern, where we left them without finding out how they were. Nothing I want is expensive."

"Dignity's very expensive," said Mr. Mapworth, "and overrated, too."

"All right, I'll let that one go. Probably way too late for it anyway. Sir, what I don't want is for your daughter to have absolute power over me. She's made my life a living hell since I arrived on this planet. I want something better than terror and slavery."

"That sounds reasonable," said Mr. Mapworth.

"I understand you can promise me anything, and there's no way I can make you keep your promise." He shrugged again. "In the local power hierarchy, I'm screwed. Still, I'd like some kind of promise, a show of good will, something."

"I'll make you a junior partner in Cavern Enterprises," said Mr. Mapworth. "You won't own any stock to start with, but

I'll give you an office and a salary, with escalating bonuses if you produce. I'll consult you on cavern matters as necessary, if what Histly says is right, and you have an ambassadorial in with the aliens. I reward skill and ability, and I think you might develop in interesting ways. If you don't, I reserve the right to cut you loose with no benefits, though, and hand you over to Histly."

"You heard that, Histly," Kaslin said. "For about two seconds, I have a title."

She nodded. "I heard. I'll honor it. You should know I'm a senior partner, though."

"But Mr. Mapworth is more senior than you."

"Yes. At this time, that's true."

"I can appeal to him, he can give you an order, and you'll follow it? Like, I can ask him to ask you to quit pestering me, and you'll do it?"

"Define 'pester.'"

Kaslin looked at Mr. Mapworth.

"We all know what Davorna means by pester, Histly. Stifle your worst impulses and cut the boy some slack."

"All right," said Histly. Then, in a whisper, "For now."

Probably as good as it was going to get. "Thank you, sir. Thanks, Histly." Kaslin took a deep breath and stood up. He emptied one of his pockets onto the table, lifted a handful of powder, patted it flat. "Histly's right about this being many different things. Food, tools, wall, floor, powder, solid, sticky stuff. Blook blook blook." He turned his hand over and let the hardened disk fall onto his supper plate. It landed with a solid thwack and broke the plate.

Histly took some of the powder in her hand. "Blook blook

blook," she whispered to it, rubbed a finger through it. Still powder.

"Okay," said Kaslin. "That's interesting. When I first went down there—before I got bleached and hairless—I heard voices. When I repeated what they said, this stuff performed for me. I was still fully human." He picked up the disk and binked it until it shone brighter than the lights in the table. Then he dimmed its light and bukked it back into powder. It was essentially the same demonstration he'd done for his mother, but she had been able to make things work, too.

Mr. Mapworth held out a hand. "Show me."

Kaslin dropped powder into Mr. Mapworth's hand, blooked it hard without touching it. Mr. Mapworth frowned, picked up the solid with his other hand, turned it over to look at a pressed map of his own palm. His eyes lit up. "This is going to be—oh, this is going to be big. Light it."

Kaslin binked, and the stone in Mr. Mapworth's hand lit, pink spots that spread and connected as he repeated the word.

"Some of it hardened, and some of it didn't. Some of it lit and the rest didn't." Fidi stirred the leftover powder on the table with her finger. "So it does things because you want it to?"

"Maybe."

"We have to get you into the lab," said Mr. Mapworth.

"He doesn't want to be dissected," said Histly.

"Who would? Not to dissect, but we have to quantify these things so we can figure out how to replicate them. There are lots of ways we can examine him without cutting into him." Mr. Mapworth frowned. "What is it about your voice that works when other people's voices don't?"

"Is that even the deciding factor?" Fidi asked. "Maybe the

aliens decided to give him power over their stuff. Maybe their stuff decides who it wants to obey."

"Anyway, that's how I got Histly out of the wall. I talked the wall into being less solid, and dug her out," Kaslin said.

"Where does this stuff come from?" asked Mr. Mapworth. "Who produces it? Is it industrial or organic?"

"No information yet," said Kaslin.

Histly said, "It might be a limited resource, even though it looked like it was everywhere down there."

"We need to map the caverns and establish protocols," muttered Mr. Mapworth. "How we deal with the aliens, how we deal with the material. I want to bring some people in on it right away. We're going to need legal, xenos, and R&D on site tomorrow."

"My mom and her partner were down there."

"Your mother and her partner?"

"Yeah. My mom's a med tech and so's her partner, Avari. We left them under alien control underground. I couldn't locate them before Histly and I left. My first priority is locating them, and rescuing them if they need it."

"I agree," said Mr. Mapworth. "We've got to get them out of there before they further contaminate the site. Then we can decide how to restrict who can go into the cavern and who can't. I better get security involved in roping it off, or we'll have industrial spies invading before we know it."

Kaslin kept his peace. He didn't care why Mr. Mapworth agreed with him, as long as he agreed.

"Will you go to my lab now?" Mr. Mapworth asked.

"Dad," said Histly. "I think we can learn everything we need to later. We've been through kind of a harrowing day. I know I could use some sleep."

"We could test you while you sleep," Mr. Mapworth said to Kaslin.

"No, thanks."

Mr. Mapworth turned to his wife.

"The aviary," she said.

Mr. Mapworth nodded. "We'll put you in the aviary for now."

The aviary? Didn't that have something to do with birds? Were they putting him in a cage? Should he fight this one or wait until after he'd had some sleep? How was he going to sleep in a cage full of birds?

"Fidi," said Ms. Mapworth, "would you show our guest his room?"

"I can do it," said Histly.

"I have a few more questions for you, partner," said Mr. Mapworth to Histly.

Kaslin wondered if he should stick around and find out what that was about, but decided retreating while it was possible was better. Fidi took his hand.

"By the time you wake, we'll have body makeup and a wig for you," said Ms. Mapworth.

"Thanks," Kaslin said. Huh? "Huh?" he said.

"You cannot go out again looking as you do. It's bound to excite too much comment. We don't want people speculating on what's happened to you. You've probably already been obvious somewhere; tell me where so I can start damage control," said Ms. Mapworth.

"The only person who's seen me, aside from you and my mom and her partner, well, and the aliens, is an old guy named Dilly who works at the distillery."

"I'll get started on containing that," said Ms. Mapworth.

Kaslin studied her expressionless face. "Don't hurt him," he said, even though he knew there was no way he could stop her from doing anything she liked. He should never have named names. "He helped me. Please don't hurt him."

A small smile touched her mouth. "We have many ways to accomplish goals, young creature. Hurting people is a last resort."

Fidi's hand slid into Kaslin's. He glanced at her. "Come on," she whispered.

He let her lead him away. Despite the mysterious and mostly unknown powers of his new body, he felt tired.

He counted three more scans, sizzling jolts to his system, as Fidi led him over thresholds farther into the penthouse. Each time he jerked to a stop, she turned, startled. Then she glanced at the thresholds and shook her head. "Sorry. I forgot," she said. "Such a normal thing around here."

"Maybe the aliens can modify me again," Kaslin muttered, "so I don't notice. I wish I could communicate with them directly."

"I want to see them. Histly's repro didn't show much detail."

"I don't think you should meet them until we get the language down. You don't want the full body treatment, do you?" He stared down at his ghost-white hand in hers, then let his gaze wander up along his ropy, hairless arm to his chest. He was a stencil, a cutout against the warm amber walls, too weird for these surroundings.

"They didn't do it to Histly," she said.

"They did it to Mom."

"They did?" Fidi paused in the middle of a greenhouse room,

lots of Terra plants, ceiling panels that let in tinted sunlight, a slightly cooler color than the unrestrained version outside. The plants were a color of green he wasn't used to anymore, even though Hitherto had been terraformed in Old Earth's image, for the most part. Kaslin had become accustomed to the purple or lavender undertone in the armored leaves of Chuudoku's plants. He touched the leaf of a philodendron and thought of his last glimpse of his final baby plant as it wandered off into pale-floored darkness. A twinge of longing flashed through him. Then he got mad at himself. How could he miss the little parasite? Was it some residual plant-induced brain chemistry?

He wondered if he'd ever see any of the baby plants again. He had never gotten a good look at them. Had they found places to root? Would they be all right underground, without sunlight?

What the hell. If it was plant-induced brain chemistry, it still felt real.

"The aliens transformed your mom, too?" Fidi asked.

"Last time I saw Mom, she was as maggoty as I am," Kaslin said.

Fidi gripped his hand and stepped close to him, stood on tiptoe to whisper in his ear. "If you can, warn her away when you get down there. Tell her to hide. Dad didn't make any agreements with her. He won't be nice if he doesn't have to."

Maybe they'd cut Mom up if they caught her. "Thanks," he whispered back.

"Kiss me," she hissed.

"What?"

"There are cameras everywhere. Give them a reason for me to get this close to you."

"Histly'll kill me if I kiss you."

"She didn't before."

"Yeah, but she told me to do it that time. Anyway, it felt really weird. I like you a lot more than I like anybody else in your family, but I think I have something going on with Histly."

"Come on, Kaslin, you *hate* her."

"Sure, sort of, most of the time, but I still can't cheat on her."

Fidi growled in his ear, then kissed him on the cheek and dropped down off her toes. "Come on," she said, her tone impatient. She jerked him forward.

One more sizzling scan, a hallway with livetime walls that showed an ice planet cavern—stalactites, stalagmites, frozen lakes, tunnels with flickers of activity in them—and Fidi opened a door in one of the stalagmites into a room full of birds.

She dragged him in before he could back away. The scan on this threshold was the most intense yet. He stood while the leftover jolts jerked his muscles. A few final shudders, and he could see again.

Bigger-than-life birds perched on trees all around the center of the room, which held a round pouf of conformobed and a small table with an extensor lamp in its center. All the birds stared at him and Fidi. Some of them screeched, and a few took off. They didn't fly across the room—he noticed the floor was free of bird shit. They flew around the edges. He realized they were a livetime projection, too. "Can they see us?" he whispered.

"Yeah. It's one of Daddy's experiments. Two-way livetime. The environment reacts to you. They can't touch you, of course."

He took two steps farther into the room, and a bunch of

the largest birds, messy-feathered dark things about his size, with long beaks, squawked and dived at him. For a moment he thought they would hit him, so deft was the illusion, but they vanished instead, then reappeared across the room, screeching.

"What planet are they from?"

"Seconir. Those ones are the worst. They eat everything else in the aviary. Daddy has to keep replacing the lesser birds. You do look kind of wormy, sort of like their natural prey."

"Great guest room," Kaslin muttered.

"It's where Daddy and Mother usually put their business rivals." She strolled over to one of the trees, even though many of the birds started screaming. Some flew away, though they couldn't get far. Beyond them, Kaslin saw a cage surround. The light on the birds was artificial, not sunlight. They were probably somewhere nearby, maybe even in the same time zone. He wondered if the room ever got dark. Did the birds ever get any sleep?

"Here's your fresher," said Fidi. She touched a knot on the tree's trunk, and a door slid up, showing a normal-looking refresher stocked with everything necessary for elimination and cleansing. Its walls were mercifully free of livetime anything; they were pale aqua.

Fidi turned to another tree and pressed a knothole. Behind that door was a closet full of different-sized coveralls in pastel colors. "Your clothes," she said. "Have a good night. Once I leave, the door won't open until a family member opens it."

"You're just going to leave me here? You're a lot more like your sister than I thought."

She walked right up to him and pulled his head down, whispered, "How could you start anything with Histly?"

"She started it. Well, the aliens started it for us, but she followed up."

"Why didn't you start something with me first? Why didn't you ever want me?"

"Want you?" he whispered. "I was happy to have you for a friend. It never occurred to me you liked me some other way. Nobody ever has."

"You're such an idiot."

"More true every day," he said. "I'm sorry, Fidi. Anyway, Histly told me if I even looked at anybody else, she'd scratch their eyes out. You know more about her fingernails than I do."

Fidi growled and shoved him away from her. "You're so stupid."

"No argument."

She went to another of the trees, ignored the birds squawking at her. She touched something that didn't look any different from any other part of the tree trunk, and a panel opened. "Here's the off switch for the livetime feed," she muttered. "Mother and Daddy'll know if you turn it off, though, and I'll get in trouble for showing it to you."

Kaslin joined her, looked at the sensidot control panel. "Is there a volume control?"

"Yeah." She showed him the slider. "That's as much as I can tell you now, Kas. There's no way I can leave the door unlocked."

"It's all right," he said.

"So. You all set?"

"I guess."

"Good night, then."

"Good night, Fidi."

She opened the door—another tree trunk access—glanced at him over her shoulder, and then vanished as the door clunked shut.

Kaslin sat on the bed. The Seconir birds stared at him. They were making grinding noises in their throats. He got up and turned off the room's volume, then went into the bathroom and took a hot shower. Plenty of heat, and the soap smelled like a mixture of spices he liked. No hair to wash. Kind of liberating. Drying off in the hotbox took half the time it usually did. There was a brown unitard on a hook on the wall. He tried it on. It was built for a woman—no genital support, and extra room in the chest—but he didn't care. It was clean, and it covered him from neck to wrists to ankles. He folded his filthy cargo pants and put them carefully in a cupboard. His food supply was still in the pockets, and the unitard didn't have any pockets for him to transfer it to.

The bed had a thin blanket. He rolled up in it, hiding even his head, and fell asleep.

Someone poked Kaslin's shoulder.

He opened eyes slowly, blinking against too-bright light, even filtered through a black veil that was the blanket he'd wrapped himself in. He had to blink hard three times before he clicked back into normal vision. So the acute cave vision was his default setting now? That would get old fast.

On the other hand, after a moment of disorientation, he felt wide awake, which was different—usually it took him half an hour to reenter the waking world after being asleep. He smelled all sorts of things—the spicy scent of the soap he'd used last night, the laundry smell of the unitard and the blanket—some kind of detergent that smelled like citrus—a general air in the room that was both flavorless and warm, and a medley of scents he associated with Histly: her body scent, in his memory from both taste and smell, the vanilla deodorant she used to mask it, a faint tang that told him she'd eaten both meat and milk the night before and her body was processing it.

Weird. He couldn't remember if he'd gotten all these scent cues the day before. If he had, he had probably ignored them in the flood of other information.

"Come on, Kas. Wake up," said Histly, poking him again, but not with anything other than her fingers.

"What time is it?" he asked from inside the cocoon of blankets.

"Early. Around four A.M. It took me a while to disable all the surveillance equipment in here."

He unrolled the blanket from his head and looked up at her. The conformobed had shaped to hold him curled up, and it took a minute for the memory foam to figure out he wanted to shift positions. "You want to talk about something private?"

"Talk? Shove over." She gave him a push that rolled him over on his stomach, and flopped down beside him on the bed.

He rolled half over again and looked at the walls. Were the birds still awake?

They were gone. The livetime display showed a night forest, no artificial light in the environment at all. Details were dark. Shadow leaves rustled, and a bird called from somewhere. Peeplerts gronked from a trickling stream beyond the range of sight.

A light shone down directly on the bed from overhead, not part of the livetime broadcast. Kaslin frowned.

"Hey," Histly said. "Come on. You couldn't have liked those birds, could you? I didn't want them watching us."

"Watching us do what?"

"Quit being dense." She pulled him toward her and pressed her mouth gently to his, worked her hands into the blanket and spread it open. Her hands danced over the unitard. She lifted her mouth in midkiss, just when he had started enjoying it, and said, "What the hell is this thing? How do I get into it?"

He laughed and sat up, stripped off the unitard, floated the blanket above them so it settled over them both. He couldn't quite believe she was here and she was after him, but he didn't plan to fight her, either. She wriggled out of her clothes and pulled him on top of her. He let her lead the way; it worked well enough. She was anxious for him inside her, and he was ready for it. He managed to wait until she was shuddering under him before he exploded.

Afterward he lay across her, and she lay as still as he'd ever known her. He was afraid to move for fear of turning her into Dark Histly. He couldn't believe she was happy about her unnatural attraction to him. Pretty soon now she should be attacking him for making her feel whatever she felt, he figured. Enjoy the quiet.

"Do it again," she whispered in his ear.

To his surprise, that turned out to be possible.

Her wrist chrono alarmed them out of sound, spooned sleep. Histly groaned and gently disengaged. "I gotta get out of here before Daddy figures out about the loop I left on the surveillance." She kissed him and eased out from under the blanket, collected her clothes, opened the room's control panel and restored the birds—volume up again, and the Seconirs anxious to dive at him—and slipped out the door.

He felt rested and ready to wake, so he went back into the bathroom and took another shower. He dug his pants out of the cubby where he'd stored them the previous night and discovered that he had put them in the laundry by mistake. The pants were pristine, all their tears mended. All the precious contents of his pockets had disappeared.

His stomach immediately raged with hunger. He groaned and drank water to quiet it, which sort of worked. Then he went to the closet to check out the clothing options. Most of the pastel coveralls were too big or too small. He found a skintight pink one that fit. He put it on and pulled his cargo pants on over it. He'd restock the pockets as soon as he got back to the cave.

While he'd been in the shower, the bed had restored itself. He sat on it and tried to ignore the constant attack feints of the Seconirs. He wished he had something to study. If he were home, he'd be taking a last look at all the homework he'd covered the night before for school. He was still looking for a definite career direction before the gov assigned one to him. Well, maybe that wasn't a concern any longer, though he wondered what his actual work would be now that Histly owned him.

Did she consider their encounter last night part of his job? God, he hoped not. Or maybe he should hope for it. At least he was good enough at it that she hadn't screamed at him afterward.

The door to outside zipped open. Ms. Mapworth stood on the threshold. "Glad you're up. Come with me."

He followed her down another hall into another bedroom. This one had no livetime display; the walls were shadowy dark red, and the furniture was flowered. "Strip," said Ms. Mapworth.

7

"WHAT?" He hadn't wanted to talk with her. This might be even more of a problem.

"Strip. I didn't have time to rig you your own makeup alcove. You'll have to use mine."

"Oh." He got out of his clothes, watched a faint blush travel across his chest. He held the folded clothes in front of his groin.

Ms. Mapworth seemed completely uninterested in his nakedness. She opened a door using a handle instead of a sensidot pad, stood with it open, the knob in her hand. "I don't know what your skin looked like before, and there isn't time to find out, so I ordered the cover rather than the skinbake for your tan. Give me those clothes. Stand in here completely still with your eyes shut, feet apart, arms a little away from your sides, and try not to breathe." She gestured.

He went into the alcove and stood as she had instructed. The door closed. He saw light through his closed eyelids, felt a tingle across his skin, heard hissing and another tingle, this one more intense and cold; something was spraying on him. Something came out of the walls afterward, robot hands tipped with soft cloths, and rubbed him all over. They withdrew and the box got hot. He felt the coating on his skin harden and tighten.

Presently the door opened again, displaced air and the invasion of Ms. Mapworth's musky scent. "You may open your eyes," she said. "Much better."

He blinked and looked down at himself. No longer ghost white, with traceries of veins and arteries visible. He looked more like a doll, plastic, all one color everywhere, and no hair. The color was a nice toasty tan, though. Darker than his usual skin color.

Ms. Mapworth handed him his clothes. "Get dressed and follow me," she said.

He did. She led him into a small room off her bedroom. The walls were all mirrors and lights. She seated him on a stool in the middle of the room, tapped a drawer open, took out a stylus. "What color hair did you have? How long was it?"

"Brown." He indicated shoulder length. "Wavy."

"Close your eyes." She put her hand under his chin and tilted his head back. He sat still while she drew eyebrows above his eyes with the stylus. She used something else to glue eyelashes along his upper and lower eyelids, then ran some kind of warm instrument over his cheeks and lips. "You may open now."

He blinked and saw himself reflected, back and front into infinity. He looked like an idealized version of himself; his cheeks and lips pinker than the rest of his face; his eyebrows were broad and perfect, without the little split scar in the right one from the time he'd been pushed over onto a rock. His eyes looked startlingly blue-green in his now-dark face, with the surround of little dark lashes.

Ms. Mapworth, who'd left the room, came back with a brown-haired wig over her hand. She settled it on his head, brushed it out, paused and looked at his reflection, her own image behind him. "Why, you're actually a well-favored child, though too thin," she said, surprised.

"Thank you," he said.

"I can improve anything I set my mind to." She smiled at herself.

"Thank you again," said Kas.

"You're ready for breakfast. Come."

He followed her from the room.

They wound through a different route in the penthouse on their way back to the dining room. Kaslin only got jolted twice, once on the threshold to the dining room, and this time not quite as intensely.

Fidi, Histly, and Mr. Mapworth were already in their places. Ms. Mapworth swept into the room and gestured Kaslin forward. He stopped and posed, feet apart, arms half-lifted, feeling it was part of his job.

"Wow," said Fidi.

Kaslin glanced at Histly and dropped his arms. She had mated with his maggot self, and even seemed to enjoy it. Would she like this change?

"Nice, Mother," said Histly. "I wonder if it's going to interfere with his ambassadorship, though. Will the aliens know it's him?"

"Take the maxiscoot," Ms. Mapworth said, as she settled on her stool and programmed breakfast. "It has a makeup alcove. You can undo it all when you get there, if you must."

Kaslin wandered over and slumped onto the stool he had

sat on the night before. His stomach was a vast wasteland. Food appeared on the mealspot. He ate hot grain porridge. It quieted his hunger a little, but no longer satisfied him the way the soap flakes did. He could tell he was missing something. He tried fruit and protein strips, but they didn't satisfy him either.

"My lab workers have been studying your scans all night," Mr. Mapworth said to Kaslin when everyone had pretty much finished eating. "I want you to stop in the lab before we go survey the caverns. There are some scans we can only do there. Let's give them data before anything else about you changes, all right? Give them urine and blood specimens, too."

Kaslin shrugged.

The lab was in the building's basement. Histly and Fidi rode down the elevator with Kaslin and Mr. Mapworth; Ms. Mapworth stayed in the penthouse. The lab was vast and white, with many workstations, some enclosed and some communal. There were a lot of big machines; they were the only colorful things in view. All the scientists wore white or pastel coveralls. Some of them wore protective gear. Some of the minirooms were enclosed in clear protective plastic. Things involving flame-throwers were happening in one of them.

Mr. Mapworth led the three of them to another room and introduced Kaslin to a small, dark-haired woman. "This is Dr. Junichiro," he said. "She'll be your primary contact here. She's going to do all your workups."

"I'm excited to meet you," said the doctor. She pumped his hand. "You look different now."

"It's makeup," Kaslin said. He wondered when she'd seen him before. All that surveillance, probably.

"Lie here, please."

Kaslin lay on a sliding slab and she slid him inside a tunnel of a machine.

Manacles slid up and braceleted his wrists and ankles. A restraint extruded from the slab, eased over his forehead, and locked his head down. Another went around his waist.

"It is very hard to keep still enough," said the doctor, "so these things will help you for a little while. Don't worry. Only a little while. Close your eyes. We are doing a deep scan."

Kaslin sighed and closed his eyes. Energy jolted through him; if he hadn't been restrained, he would have jerked and struggled against it. He could only whimper.

"Stop it, Dad! Jun, stop it!" Histly said, somewhere far away. But it didn't stop for what felt like a long time.

Eventually, though, the jolting sizzle subsided. His hands unclenched. He was drenched with sweat. The slab slid out of the tunnel, and only then did the restraints come undone. He was too exhausted to move.

"Curious," said the doctor. "Reaction out of all proportion to actual test."

"He's hypersensitive to scanning," said Histly. "Don't do that again. You okay, Kas?" She took his hand, helped him sit up. His legs and arms trembled. He looked at the backs of his hands. The makeup was still there, still doing its job of making him look better than normal.

"Pretty shaky," he muttered to Histly.

"If you hurt him in any way, I'll have you blacklisted," Histly said to the doctor.

"Ms. Etasha! Ms. Etasha, this scan is never known to harm anyone!"

"He's not like anyone else on the planet," Histly said. "You don't know what will hurt him anymore. If you hear him cry out, stop what you're doing and leave him alone. Do you understand?"

The doctor looked to Mr. Mapworth, who gave her a discreet hand signal. "I understand," she said.

"I'll be fine once I get some real food," Kaslin muttered.

"Real food?"

He eased his hands into his pockets, pulled them taut to show their emptiness. "Your cleaning service ate all the rest of my food."

"Daddy?"

"The pants were processed down here. We have all the samples that were in the pockets. Davorna, are you dependent on that stuff for survival now?"

"I don't know, sir. It seems so. Your breakfast didn't feed my real hunger."

"Can you walk?"

He took in breath and pulled himself to his feet. He felt better; the queasy weakness faded out of his muscles. "Yes," he said.

"Follow me."

They crossed the lab to a different section, where workers were performing experiments on white things. "Vachel? Give me your specimen," Mr. Mapworth said to one of the workers.

"Sir?" She handed over a small box.

"Don't worry. We'll get more." He touched a sensidot on the box and the lid opened. He handed it to Kaslin.

White powder, more than a handful. Kaslin tipped the box toward his mouth, felt flakes sift onto his tongue, waited for whatever taste he would experience.

Sawdust. No flavor. No softening or change at all.

He coughed, poured some of the flakes onto his hand. "Blook blook blook," he whispered. Nothing happened. "Sir, these are dead."

"What? What have you done to them, Vachel?"

"Tested them for nanoactivity. Standard tests, sir, that we perform on all new substances you send us. From the information you sent with the samples, we suspected there would be some kind of nanotech, but nobody's been able to raise so much as a shift in electricity in any of it. The properties don't map to any substance we've seen before, but this is completely inert."

Kaslin felt the energy draining out of the soles of his feet. He sagged.

Histly caught him. "Come on, Daddy. Time to survey our purchase." She looped her arm around Kaslin, half-carried him to the elevator.

"This is a setback," said Mr. Mapworth as the four of them rode the elevator up to the groundfloor garage.

"It just means there's more to learn before we can use the new discovery," said Histly. Kaslin leaned on her arm, grateful for her support. He wondered if he'd die without cave food. He felt wilty; his mind was drifting.

He didn't focus on the ride to the cavern in the maxiscoot. There were many people along, and someone told him who they were, but he didn't retain any of it. Histly's arm was warm and strong around him. Her smell reassured him. Fidi sat across from him, staring at his face. He kept his eyes closed so he wouldn't see her concentration, but he could still smell her, in the mass mixture of people and cleaning smells inside the car.

When the car stopped, Histly urged him to climb on her back. He did it without hesitation. She strode off through the spike trees without waiting for anyone, and when they came to the cave opening, she lay down on the ground, unhooked his arms from around her neck, and eased him in. "Go on," she whispered, and gave him a push.

He crawled across the floor until he reached the flakes. As soon as his hands touched them, he felt stronger. He scrambled over them until he reached the first slope, then plunged down. At the bottom, he said, "Bike," and the floor rose up and wrapped around him. He lay in its embrace, breathing strength in and weakness out. A wave of floor rose up, trickled itself into his open mouth. Salty dried meat he could chew. With every swallow, his energy returned.

"Hey!" Histly yelled, somewhere outside his walls. "No. Don't. Leave me alone!"

Kaslin stood up. The wrappings around him fell away into powder. He shoveled it into his pockets until they bulged.

The aliens had returned, and they had Histly in their grip. There were a lot of them, more than he'd seen in one gathering before. They were pulling Histly flat, the way they had with his mother and Avari, exploring the fastenings of her clothes.

He jumped to his feet and ran to them. "Bootah," he said.

"Bootah," they responded.

He tugged on one of the flower hands holding Histly's leg. He needed language, but he didn't have it. "Bik lily," he said.

They broke into a chorus of "boo boo boo!" and let Histly go. She staggered, straightened, and ran to him, crouched behind him so she could press herself to him, her arms around his torso, her face against his shoulder and neck. Shudders wracked her.

She was breathing nearly silent sobs.

"Bootah," Kaslin said, relieved.

"Bootah," said the one nearest Kaslin, and its hands explored his face, tugged on his hair until the wig came off. It showed its trophy to the others. One or two tasted the fake hair. More of them laughed. One handed the wig back. Another took his hand and licked the back of it, lifted the makeup off and left a swathe of ghost skin. It spoke rapidly to the others.

They descended on him and licked his head and hands until he was pale again in all the places not covered by his clothes. He let his arms go limp to give them free access. Their tongues were efficient and stimulating. Histly clung to him from behind, and they left her alone, except to shift her head to give them access to the bare skin of the back of his neck. "Buh," one murmured in his ear after they had stopped licking him.

"Okay, I'm sorry. I won't cover up again if it bothers you. There are some adjustments I'd like you to make, though."

"Ub ub ub?" It was the first questioning tone he'd heard from them. Words from one of the elementary first contact manuals he had read came back to him: "Never assume the Other is reacting the way a human would. Wait for context to make the Other's actions clear, and even then, question and doubt your conclusions. We cannot understand the Other without prolonged observation and willing exchange of information. Nevertheless, begin collecting information as soon as possible. Each piece of information you collect will shift your relationship to all the other pieces. Be prepared to have your expectations overturned again and again."

Just thinking about prolonged observation and withholding conclusions until he'd collected more information made him tired. Anyway, these aliens didn't run a first contact the way any of the example species sims in the manual did. They weren't waiting for him to figure them out before they took action.

"Did you make it so I can't survive outside the caverns? That sucks! Why can't I live on any food I can eat? Do you want me to die? Or do you just want me to be trapped down here forever?"

A storm of conversation rose among them.

"Do they understand you?" Histly whispered.

"I don't know. I'm venting," he whispered back.

An interruption came from up the chute. People on snowslider boards shot down, one right after another. "Bike!" cried the aliens. "Bike! Bike! Bike!" One by one, the new arrivals were swallowed by the floor, forming lumps of white. One of the aliens broke loose of the crowd around Kaslin and Histly and ran over to the new lumps, repeating, "Bike!" until the lumps grew larger. "Blook," said the alien. Then, "Bikit bikit bikit." The group around them repeated a chorus of "Bikit!"

"Bikit?" Kaslin said. A bristly hand tapped his lips. A forbidden word?

"Four, five, six, seven," Histly breathed near his ear. "Yep. That's everyone else."

"Everyone?"

"There were nine of us in the scoot," she said.

"I was too out of it to notice."

"Daddy and Fidi should be able to fight free. They have the same augmentations I do."

"This time it's different."

She straightened behind him, loosed her hold a little, leaned forward. She stared over his shoulder toward the mounds. They watched as time went by. No movement. No sounds.

"Breathing room," she said.

One alien stood guard over the mounds. All the rest turned their attention back to him.

"Ub?" said the one who had touched his mouth.

"Should I have asked you before I brought other people down here?" he said.

"Negev," said someone.

"Bishilly loohah," said someone else.

"Good, because they do things without me being able to stop them. I'm honored you chose me to—I don't know what it is you chose me for, but you treat me better than you treat the others. I can't control the rest of my race. I don't know that I'm a good ambassador for you. They don't listen to me. Most of them have more power than I do. You should have picked somebody with more power on the outside."

"Bootah bist."

"Bootah," he said. "I have to bring a scribe next time. I want to make a dictionary."

"Beh," said one of them, and stroked a hand over his head, down his shoulder: soothing. "Belily anoktik." Others touched him, tugged at his clothes.

Several of them grasped Histly's arms, loosened her hold on him, pulled her away. She wailed.

"Wait," he said. "Don't—don't do anything to her, okay? You wanted us together, we're together. Leave her alone."

Three of them held her, many flower hands on her arms and legs. She turned her head and looked at them. They didn't let go, nor did they do anything else to her. "It's okay," she said in a choked voice. A fourth stroked a hand over her head, patted her shoulder: the same pattern of soothing they had used on him. If soothing was what they were doing. "It's okay, Kas. They're not hurting me."

The others closed around him so he couldn't see her anymore, a thicket of limbs and bodies. They reached for him, worked the stiktites on his pants and pulled them off, figured out how to get him out of the coverall. They held him up between them, arms and legs extended, parallel to the ground. He sighed, remembering other sessions like this.

First they examined him, with eyes and the flower stalks around their faces, which swiveled and scanned. They ticked at the sight of his almost-all-over body makeup. Two licked it, lifting tongue-shaped strips from him and leaving pale behind.

"Bizilly," said one of them. His skin shivered, flared with electric fire. The makeup peeled off in curling strips and dropped to the floor. The heat faded as soon as he was clean.

"Whoa," Kaslin said. "Bizilly?" A flush swept over him, hot and strange, subsided. It scared him. They could speak and make him change, the way they made the wall stuff change? Other people could tell his body to do things, and it would, without his permission? He could tell himself to do things. Weird.

What Fidi had said: words didn't work for everyone. Something was deciding who could make the words work. Maybe it wasn't him, though.

The aliens laughed, a mixed chorus of boos. Then, still holding him extended and helpless, they examined him, their faces an inch from his skin, their flowers more active than he'd seen them before. "What?" he said.

"Justnets," said one of them.

"What?"

A tongue arrowed toward his stomach and opened a long, deep slice from his groin up to his chest; he could see his internal organs, glistening and pulsing. He screamed.

8

ONE OF THE ALIENS packed the cut with floor flakes. Kaslin realized there was no pain, and no blood jetting from the cut.

"Are you all right?" Histly cried from somewhere near.

"I don't know," he said, his voice high and panicked.

"Justnets," said someone else.

"Food," said another. Tongues worked in the wound. No blood shot out, and he could barely feel what they were doing. So many of their heads hovered over him he couldn't see past them.

"Oh," he said. Food. They had spoken in Standard. Food. They had understood his request for adjustments? They were taking him seriously? "Oh. Thank you. Avoz. If you can do that, can you make it so it doesn't hurt me every time a scanner goes through me?"

"Escanner?" asked one of the ones not operating on him.

"It's a machine they use to look inside me. I don't know how it works. Some kind of radiation or emission. I feel it every time, and they keep doing it. It wipes me out."

"Bedu," said one, and another storm of conversation ran through them.

A tongue tapped his forehead and knocked him out.

*

He woke up in a pit with Histly. She had her arms and legs wrapped around him, holding him with his bare belly against hers. She was also asleep.

He was warm, and all around him were soft fluffy flakes, a cushion of them, a blanket of them. He rolled his head and looked up: above, far above, a ceiling of some sort, scattered with faint spots of yellow and green light in groupings. "Bink," he whispered. "Bink bink bink." Pink light bloomed in the nearby walls of the pit. He and Histly were in the bottom of a hole in the cavern floor, buried in soft flakes, only their heads exposed. He closed his eyes and listened to himself. He felt good all through. Histly's arms and legs and front were warm against him, but not threatening. Her breathing was soft and slow, easing past his cheek in waves. She still looked tan and had eyebrows and most of her pink hair.

He moved his arm, worked his hand up between their bodies to feel his belly. Smooth, unscarred. The aliens had made adjustments, unless he'd dreamed the operation. Had they really understood his requests?

"Histly?" he whispered.

She stirred. Her eyes opened. Her arms tightened around him, then relaxed. "You okay?"

"Yeah."

"You screamed."

"They kind of cut me open."

"What?" She rubbed her eyes, then stared at him. "What?" She touched his face. "You look different."

He shifted around and sat up, shedding flakes. He stared down at his stomach, blinked twice. He wasn't ghost white any-more; his skin was back to his normal color, indoor pale but human. He ran his hands down his chest, across his stomach. No seam, no scar.

He lifted a handful of flakes and bit them. Filufa mousse, a cool, creamy fruit taste that slid across his tongue and down his throat—one of the better tastes. He could still eat and enjoy the floor; that was something, anyway.

"Share," Histly said as she sat up.

He ate more, then changed some in his mouth and kissed her. "Mm," she said. "Best yet, except for the chocolate cake." They sat waist deep in powder, eating in tandem, pausing to kiss, which eventually led to other things, until a polite cough sounded above them.

Kaslin lifted his mouth from Histly's and glanced up, to see his mother sitting on the lip of the pit, her legs dangling over the edge. She was still bald, but no longer ultra pale. She wore her inner skin, the garment that went inside her biosuit. Her feet were bare. "I think you're in the same positions you were last time I saw you," she said. "Perhaps introductions are in order now?"

"Hi, Mom. I was going to find you."

"I can tell. It was a priority, obviously."

"This is Histly Etasha."

"Hi, Histly. I'm Serena Davorna, Kaslin's mother. You're not yelling threats at my boy anymore, are you?"

"No," said Histly. "Also he told me not to use poison on him anymore. I do occasionally torture him, though, and I bought his work contract from your husband, so I own him."

"What?" His mother sounded appalled.

"Can Dad do that, Mom? Sell my work contract for six years?"

"Not without my consent," she said. "Supposedly. I would never authorize that, Kas. But the government here is so corrupt I guess there are ways around it. You must be connected, Histly."

"Her father's Peck Mapworth," Kaslin said. "Her mother's Lilia Mapworth."

"Oh, Avoz. Avoz!"

"Mr. Mapworth was buried in the floor, along with his exploration team and Histly's little sister Fidi, right after they came down here, following me. I don't know when that was."

Histly cleared powder off her wrist chrono. "About twelve hours ago. I wonder how they're doing."

"The aliens used something more intense than 'bike' to bury them. Nobody escaped right away. We should probably go check on them." Kaslin sighed. "Histly bought the caverns, Mom."

"Avoz," Serena whispered.

"But obviously I can't control the aliens," Histly said. "There are probably all kinds of treaty laws I'll have to obey once the gov finds out what we've discovered. I've staked my claim every way I could, but that may not mean anything. I can only hope."

"How's Avari, Mom?" asked Kaslin.

"Disabled," she said slowly. "I don't understand what's happening here. The aliens like me. They altered me in ways I don't yet understand—they took away my equipment, so I can't analyze myself properly, but I've been experimenting, and I've learned interesting things about my new self. They follow me around and teach me words. When I say the words, things happen to the walls. I amuse the aliens. Just recently, they altered me again."

"I asked for modifications so I can be more comfortable

outside. When I was out there, I found out I couldn't eat normal food anymore, or at least, it didn't feed me," Kaslin said. "I think the aliens gave me what I asked for. Maybe they fixed you, too."

"Do you speak their language?" asked Serena.

"Some of it. Not that I understand most of it. I think they understand us, though."

"Well, they're treating me well enough, but they imprisoned Avari. They put him in a wall and tapped his forehead, and he's been unconscious ever since. He has a bunch of augmentations that are supposed to prevent things like that—he's supposed to be patient-proof. His augmentations were designed to stop anybody else from disabling him, which is one of the reasons he makes a great partner. But the aliens—maybe he's too dangerous to them, and they only let the feeble ones run around loose."

"Do you feel feeble?" Kaslin asked. "I don't."

She smiled down at him. He considered his own words. They surprised him. He liked them. He wasn't sure he believed himself.

"Great talk for somebody at the bottom of a pit," said Histly.

"Do you want to get out?"

"Are you crazy? Of course I want to get out! But I know already it's no use trying to climb the sides of one of these things. We have to wait for the spiders."

"No, we don't." He blooked the floor until it was solid enough to stand on, then stood. He grabbed Histly's hand and pulled her to her feet. "I think if I increase the texture, we can swim up to the surface. It worked before."

"Increase the texture?" she said. She dug into the wall,

released a shower of powdery flakes. "What do you mean?"

He leaned against the wall and blooked at it. The flakes grew denser, though they didn't solidify into plate. When he sensed the conditions were right, he dived into the wall and swam toward the surface, and the white material acted semisolid enough to support him but not block him. Histly came behind him, and he felt the surrounding powder softening behind him, hardening, working against her. He spoke to it crossly, got up to the surface, blooked a solid platform to sit on, then reached down into the ground, which had closed behind him. He had to fish to find her hands and pull her out, and then she coughed and choked for a while before she found her breath. She spat out flakes.

His mother came over. Kaslin put his knees up and together and rested his hands on top, masking himself as well as he could from his mother, even though he knew she'd seen him naked. Histly, on the other hand, was not hiding anything. She was still fighting for air.

His mother offered a water bottle to Histly. Histly rinsed out her mouth and spat, then drank. "Thanks," she said at last, in a hoarse voice. "Kaslin, how could you breathe in that stuff? I have aug lungs, and even so, I almost drowned."

"I'm sorry," he said. "I didn't know it would work that way."

"It was the same for Avari," said Serena. "Our alterations make this our natural environment. You augmented guys are strangers here. Good thing we're too poor to afford augs, Kas, huh?"

"What?" He thought about all the people buried in the first cavern. Mr. Mapworth. Fidi. Augmented for sure. The five specialists? Mr. Mapworth could afford the best; probably they had all reached places in their careers where they added extra job modules and augs to shape them better for their jobs. "Wah. I wonder if that's a deciding factor."

"Just a hypothesis at this point. Maybe they like our genes better."

"For now, I'm going to stick to you," Histly said. She handed the water bottle back to Serena and scooted to Kaslin, leaned against his back, wrapped her arms around his waist from behind. "You're as close to a native guide as I want to get. The spiders make me shudder."

"Okay," he said.

His mother handed him the water, and he drank. Then he said, "You sure Avari's all right?"

"I checked his condition right before I came to find you. Buried up to the neck in white stuff, and unconscious, but breathing."

"Do you want to get him out?"

She hesitated. "He's the best partner I've ever had. Yet it's kind of restful not to have to deal with him. He hacked the locators all right, and got us off the grid, but he keeps wanting to call somebody in authority and tell them what's going on. I'm not ready to summon the government. I'm hoping to find out more about what makes our new friends do the things they do. This is a researcher's paradise. I'd just as soon leave him to sleep, if I can be sure he's all right."

"I think the aliens know us pretty well," Kaslin said. "I bet Avari's fine. Did you watch when they did surgery on you?"

"Watch? I was unconscious."

"I saw them working on me. Unnerving. Maybe unsanitary. Deft, though. No hesitations." He ran a hand from his chest to his groin. "No scars."

"They actually cut you open? What kind of tools did they

use? Was anesthesia involved? I've been assuming they took us somewhere while we were out and operated on us there, with some kind of fantastic technology we've never heard of. I haven't seen any equipment anywhere, and no labs, even though I've been wandering around the caverns for hours. All the rooms are a different shape. All of them are coated in this warm ice. None of the aliens wears clothing or carries any tools. I just thought they were hiding the real working caverns really well."

"Have you considered the mutability of the white stuff?" Kaslin asked.

"Of course."

"It's the tools. It's everywhere. You can make it do whatever you want. I think they have hands with specialized functions, too. And their tongues have…um…capabilities ours don't have. The surgery was all performed with tongues. The part I was awake for, anyway."

"Hmm," said his mother. "They're their own toolkits? Kaslin, I like the way your mind works. I hope you'll choose a research career module when we can afford it. Isn't that where you want to be?"

"I don't know. I always dreamed about working in alien contact."

She laughed. "I knew that, but I thought you'd figure out that opportunities in the field are limited, especially if you're entrenched here on Chuudoku, which we are, with the articles and covenants we had to sign to get here. We're tied up for the next ten years, at least. How wrong I was. Now that you've made first contact, don't you want to research everything associated with it?"

Kaslin thought about it. "I'm not sure. First I want to find out if I can eat human food again."

Histly stirred against his back. "We could test that right away if we could find my pack. I brought foodblocks. I wonder where our stuff is? Why do they always take our clothes off?"

"When did they take off your clothes?" Kaslin asked.

"Back in the first cavern. They held me for a long time while they worked on you. It took them about three hours, I think. Next time they let go of my arms and I could check my chrono, anyway, three and a half hours had passed.

"Once they finished doing things to you, you lay there on the floor, asleep or knocked out, and they came and took all my stuff away and examined me. Not as intensely as they did the first time. I didn't fight it, and they didn't disable me, but they didn't talk to me, either, even though I kept asking them what they had done to you. They picked us both up and carried us a long way, then one of them dug this hole and they lowered us both down into it. You wouldn't wake up. I was afraid to hurt you, so I didn't shake you or anything. I tried climbing out, but it was the same as the first time; every time I clawed at the walls, I just made the pit wider and buried us in flakes. Eventually I decided to go to sleep. I'm glad you woke up."

"Me, too," he said.

Histly said, "Miz Davorna, how'd you get your clothes back from them?"

"My things were in the first cavern, where I lost them," Serena said. "I found my way back."

"Maybe my stuff is still there, too," Histly said.

Kaslin wondered if his clothes had survived being taken off him. The aliens had undone the stiktites. Maybe the clothes were intact. Such as they were.

Kaslin gripped Histly's hands, unhooked her enough to

stand up. She stood before he could get to his feet, though, and brought him up with her. Standing, he was reminded again that she was taller than he was, but she didn't use her height to push him around anymore. "Let's go back. We can find our stuff and check on the exploration team."

He looked around the cavern the new pit was in. He didn't recognize any of the features. The lights were more green and yellow than pink, which reminded him of the prison tunnel where the aliens had put Histly, but this was a wider room, with a number of openings off it. He wished he had a locator he could access. He had no idea which direction to go.

"This way," said his mother, heading toward a narrow opening in a direction he had thought of as wrong. She led them into a small tunnel, binking lights as she went. Eventually, the tunnel opened into a vaster cavern. He saw a rise in the floor that reminded him of something he'd seen before, though he couldn't remember when.

"How the heck did you find us, Mom?"

"I asked the aliens where you were, and two of them led me there," she said. As she spoke, several aliens drifted up to join them. Histly put her hands on his shoulders from behind, matched her strides to his shorter ones so they could walk in lockstep.

"Bootah," Kaslin said to the aliens, and they responded with the same word. One of them touched his stomach. He stopped.

"Bilily?" it said.

"As far as I know," he answered. "Haven't had a chance to test it yet."

"Beniktok."

"I hope so. Thanks."

"Do you understand what it's saying?" Histly whispered.

"No. Just guessing," he whispered back.

One of the others tapped his mother on the head. She smiled. "Bootah," she said.

"Bootah. Bilily?"

"The girl has some regular food. If we can find her things, we can taste it and find out."

"Bedu," said the alien. Serena started walking again, and the aliens strode along with them through the cavern.

Kaslin lifted Histly's hand off his shoulder and tugged her forward, pulled her arm through his so that they walked side by side. She adjusted their arms to suit her and walked with him. He noticed her uneasy glances at the aliens, but most of the time she was looking around.

"Noticing landmarks?" he asked, in a normal voice, which startled him, Histly, and his mother.

"Trying to," said Histly. "Not so easy when everything is white."

"Not everything is," said Serena. "The lights I make are pink, but there are others in different colors. I wonder where the other kinds of lights come from."

"Mom, did I tell you I woke the aliens?"

"What? No! You haven't told me much at all."

"You woke those things up?" Histly said, her tone a return to the old days, when everything she said to him was nasty.

He decided to ignore her tone. "You didn't see them when you first got down here, did you?"

"How could I see anything? I was stuck in a hole in the ground."

"I was wandering in a tunnel after I left you, trying to figure out how to get out of the caverns, saying my new words, and I saw these dark spots in the wall. I brushed one off and found a face. I softened the wall and dug out the face, and then its eyes opened, and—"

"That was your first contact?" Serena asked.

He nodded. "It came out of the wall, all these furry legs, something huge and scary breaking free. I tried to hide in the white stuff, but they could make it do everything I could make it do, and more. They took me out again and examined me... They must have taught me all the control words before they woke up."

"How did that work?" asked his mother.

"I heard words as soon as I got down here. Something talked to me from the walls. I repeated the words I heard, and things happened. Light came. The floor got more solid, or softer. You know."

"Odd," said his mother.

"But Mom, what's weirder still, Histly can say the same words, and they don't work. When the scientists in the Mapworth labs tried to analyze the powder, it turned inert."

"You heard the words, but there were no aliens at first?" Histly asked.

"Right." Kaslin glanced at the nearest alien; the pack was drifting silently behind and to the right of the three humans, not near enough to speak with in a conversational tone, just as though they were a different species of migrating animal on the same trek. "Ub?" Kaslin said.

The alien cut across to him, walked to the side where Histly wasn't. "Ub?"

"Were you asleep until I got here?"

"Bedu." It reached out with two arms and pulled him to a stop, then wrapped him in a python embrace, more arms than he could count, and licked the top of his head. "Bedu. Rong su-reep." It unwound itself from him and ran a hand from the top of his head down his neck, along his shoulder and down his arm, an extended version of the touch he had come to call soothing.

"Why were you asleep?"

"Do you hibernate?" asked Serena.

Two more aliens approached, and then the whole herd. One emerged from the herd and stood in front of them. It blinked its third eye, the central one, and for the first time Kaslin noticed one alien was different from the others. This one's third eye had a touch of color in it, a fleck that was something more than reflected light, lighter than the surround of black. It placed a hand on Kaslin's head and spoke:

"We're a residual force, left behind on this colony planet when the others moved on. It's our practice everywhere we go to leave a few of us behind in case someone interesting shows up after we've gone. My sibs and I have waited a long time for you to find us and wake us."

"How long?" Kaslin said. He blinked, shook his head, dislodged the hand on it. What? Had he really heard and understood the alien? What?

It placed the hand on the same spot on his head and pressed. "The last time we saw your kind, you were confined to a single planet and just learning to stand upright. We made a few changes and left markers in you then. We haven't decided if we're pleased with all the results, but we're very happy with individual you."

Kaslin swallowed. If he was hallucinating, it was pretty convincing. If he wasn't, maybe he should find out as much as he could before something else happened. "You met us before?"

Serena touched his arm. "Kaslin?" she whispered. "Can you understand it?"

"Yeah, suddenly. You don't?"

"Not a word. What's it saying?"

"I'll tell you later."

The alien said, "We've met and cataloged and sometimes shifted most of life in this galaxy, one way or another. We are great explorers, those of us who have the bent, and great long-range planners and manipulators. I prefer being planetbound to exploring; this was a planet I was fond of, so I didn't mind staying when the main force left. I'm anxious to get aboveground and see which of our projects here have borne fruit during the long time we were asleep. We were thrilled when you returned with the colony plants. That was one of my projects. I'm delighted it survived and thrived. The way we shifted you worked well in concert with them. I hoped that would happen, but I couldn't be sure until I saw results."

"Where did the plants go when they left me?" Kaslin heard the plaintive note in his voice.

"It's not a dark-adapted species, child. We had to let them loose aboveground so they could get some sunlight for their next stage. I can show you where. I'm sure they'll be glad to see you." It rubbed his head. He thought it was smiling. "You haven't come into contact with bizillabex since we altered you, have you? One of my colleagues is anxious to study the outcome of that encounter."

"I don't even know what bizillabex is."

"They used to be everywhere. A single stalk, about your height, a flower at the apex, with another shooting seed, but this one symbiotes in your interior. The seed is sophisticated; it analyzes the host's degree of health, and fixes medical problems where it finds them. Sometimes it grows new organs in its hosts or introduces a second nervous system. Its interior stage can last three years, though with the way we've modified you, that stage may go faster. Satisfactory hosts survive when the embryo exits for its next stage of development. You will be a most satisfactory host. We think you may add some genetic material to the plant and change its nature in an interesting way, as you did with the colony plants."

"I what?" He hadn't heard of plants like bizillabex, and he wasn't sure what the alien meant about his changing the assassin plants. If it had happened, he hadn't done it on purpose. He wondered if the bizillabex had been lost in the terraforming. He hoped so.

Histly pulled on his arm. "What's it saying?" she whispered to him. "Tell us now."

"No. I have to ask it more questions."

Histly cuffed his head. "Your questions can wait. Don't leave us in the dark so long."

"Are you sure you want this toxic one awake?" asked the alien, whose hand still rested on top of Kaslin's head. "At first we thought your union was amusing, but we're not so sure anymore. We can remove and store her elsewhere if you want."

"No, it's all right. Don't hit me, Histly."

She sighed. "Sorry. Every once in a while I forget how things have changed. How come you can understand it and we can't?"

"Why is that?" Kaslin asked the alien.

"We are reserving communication rights with the others until we get a grasp of the current political situation," said the alien. "Various information we've gathered makes us think there may be large obstacles to navigate when we emerge and speak to the population above."

"You're not speaking Standard," he said. "How can I understand you?"

"You are our creature now, Kaslin," it said gently.

Everyone's creature but my own.

It soothed him with one hand, not taking the other hand from the top of his head. "We have made a number of modifications in you, as you know. As long as I apply pressure just here on your head, you can understand our language. If you like, I can make that modification permanent, so you can understand us without my touching you. It is your choice."

"You're not speaking Standard, but you understand it?"

"Some of us receive communications in many forms, and we've been studying all the transmissions we've collected. There's a density of communications in the world above, along many routes. We have lots of samples to work with. This is a great time to be awake, Kaslin. Thank you for finding us."

"Sure," he said. He shifted his shoulders, uncomfortable in ways he couldn't define. No time yet to sort things out. "The language," he said, then couldn't think what he wanted to say next.

"Do you want me to shift it into your brain?"

"Take your hand off."

It lifted the hand away from his head.

"Say something."

It spoke. He heard lots of b's and l's and vowel sounds. He didn't understand any of them. He reached for its hand and placed it back on his head and said, "Please. Give me that."

A faint pressure on his skull, and then it released him. He sighed. "Okay. Thanks. We're going to the other cavern to find our clothes and the other people we brought down here. Histly has some food. I thought I could try eating it and see if it nourishes me."

"It should. We didn't mean to give you such a disadvantage." The alien began walking in the direction they had been going.

"Then this—" He patted his arm, its new, more normal color.

"We didn't realize your species used visual cues that way, until you came back cloaked in false color. We didn't mean to make you look strange to your kind. We want to give you maximum functioning." It soothed him one more time. "Come. Let's test." It strode on ahead of them.

Kaslin stumbled, then walked along in its wake. Histly clung to his arm, and Serena walked with them; the other aliens kept pace.

"Tell us," Histly whispered. "What were you talking about?"

"I can't tell you now," he whispered back.

"Did it at least tell you why you can understand it?"

"They put the language in my head."

"What's a bizillabex?" Serena asked.

"Another kind of partner plant that shoots a seed into you. They want me to hook up with one. Mom, are there other partner plants?"

"There are several other kinds. Some of them are being developed into more effective bio weapons. Others already have weapons status; one of our most lucrative exports. Most of them are confined to plantations; they're too dangerous to encounter without supervision. The assassin vines, despite their name, have never actually killed anybody. At least, not anybody in range of town; we know how to treat people for assassin vine infestation. Why would they want you to be infested?"

"They're easily amused," he muttered. He strode forward and caught up with one of the aliens. "How many of you are awake now?"

"The whole outpost. We've got more than enough work for everybody; in fact, we've laid eggsacs. We need more people. This is a fertile time for study."

"What did it say?" Serena asked.

"Can you give Mom language, too?" Kaslin asked the aliens.

"No," said the alien.

"Why not?"

"As long as it's just one person, we can keep track of it. If we start spreading it out, it becomes chaotic, and right now, we need to control access."

"What's to stop me from telling Mom what you just told me?"

"Nothing," said the alien. They entered another tunnel, bunched together to travel in the narrower confines. Histly's grip on his arm tightened into punishing range.

He shifted, tugged at her hand until she loosened it. "*Shh*," he said. "It's all right. They won't hurt you."

"How can you be sure?" she whispered.

"I asked them not to."

"That works?"

"I think so."

"Why?"

"Why what? Why does it work, or why did I ask them not to?"

"Both."

"Convenience," he said, to be mean.

The tunnel opened out into another cavern. At its far side, distant and huge, stood the steep chute that led up toward the outside world. Halfway across the cavern, Kaslin saw the first pit where Histly had spent time. It was much bigger than it had been the last time he saw it. He wondered how long she had been trapped there, imprisoned in spite of her powers, struggling to get out. If he hadn't spent so much time aboveground running away from things that eventually caught him anyway, he could have let her out sooner.

By the time he came back, she had been stuck in a wall somewhere else. Maybe all that time immobilized had done her good. Maybe she meditated a little. He liked the direction their relationship had taken, but he didn't trust it to last. Once they returned to the place of her power—but that wasn't fair. When he had been weak from hunger in the place of her power, she had taken care of him. She had brought him back here, where he could recover, even though she hadn't been happy here.

She looked into the pit as they passed, then glanced away.

"I'm sorry I left you alone so long," he murmured.

"Yes, well," she said. "It's like you said. If I were you, I would have stayed away forever."

They came to the chute. "Want me to take you up?" Histly asked.

"We will carry you," said the aliens. One grabbed him, one Serena, and one Histly, who screamed and then stopped. The aliens raced up the slope to the plateau between chutes. They set the humans down by their scattered possessions.

Kaslin grabbed his body suit and pants, pulled them on. Histly slid into her clothes and fastened all the stiktites, then reached for her pack. She dug out a gourmet foodblock, hit the heating pad, and handed it to Kaslin. Even before he tasted it, he could smell the steam, redolent of spices and baking, heavy cake with fruit in it. His mouth watered. He sat on the floor and removed the outer wrapper, bit into the cake. Flavor exploded across his tongue. He chewed and swallowed, the texture a treat after the repeated pasty consistency of the powdery stuff he'd been eating. The cake went down into his stomach, and hunger eased. His body felt happy with itself and its ability to digest.

"Avoz! Thank you," he said. "Thank you, everyone, for making this possible."

Histly sat down beside him and broke off a piece of cake, ate it. "It works?"

"As far as I can tell."

"Oh, good. So I can take you places."

"Such as?" he asked, strangely tickled.

"State dinners and things like that. You'll be able to eat regular food once I teach you table manners."

He laughed, handed her the rest of the cake, stood, and wandered over to the mounds of white that buried the Mapworth exploration party. His mother followed him. One of the aliens was still guarding the mounds.

"Have they been trying to escape?" Kaslin asked.

"Several of them have remarkable resilience," said the alien, its voice a few notches lower than the other he had talked with. "We had to try several different introductions to sleep them."

"Do you know which one holds the young girl?"

The alien laid a hand on one of the mounds. "She's one of the fighters. Good breath control."

"May I let her out?"

"We would like to totally examine her," said the alien.

"She's just a kid."

It soothed him, stroked head, neck, shoulder, arm. "Not sexually mature? You worry for its mental safety."

"Yes."

The other aliens had drifted over to join them.

"We'll restrain ourselves," said one of them, "but we need to examine any of them we awake. They've altered themselves in crude ways that nevertheless give them unexpected skills and powers we need to protect ourselves against."

"Understood," Kaslin said. He knelt by Fidi's mound, put his hands on its hard surface. Histly knelt beside him. "Buk buk buk," he whispered, and felt the surface powder under his hands. He shoveled it aside, digging like a dog as he spoke it soft. Presently he uncovered Fidi, whose face was relaxed in sleep. Her hands were clenched into loose fists.

Aliens flooded into the excavation around him, lifted Fidi.

"Hey!" Histly yelled. "Don't let them—"

"They won't do it all, but they will do most of it," Kaslin said.

"Stop them, Kas. Don't let them do that to her."

"Do you want her awake? That's what it costs."

"Kas," she said, tugging on his arm. "Talk to them."

He pushed his way in among the aliens and gathered Fidi in his arms, though several of them kept their hands on her. "Please," he said. He wished he could say: If you wanted to examine her, why didn't you do it while she was asleep, before we got here? But his mother and Histly could still understand him, though they didn't yet understand the aliens. Mom would probably understand his idea of the best plan—surrender to the inevitable, get concessions where you could, pretty much what he'd practiced in regular life—but he didn't think Histly would.

"There are political aspects to this," he said to the aliens instead. "One of the people you have buried here—Histly's father, this girl's father—is one of the most powerful people on the planet."

"Good," said one of the aliens. "We can use that."

"Use it?" he said.

"We need to establish relations with your government if we want to coexist here. And we do. You will fascinate us for several generations. New things will come of this association. We can make some alterations to your friend's father that will help us deal with your government. Thank you again for acting as interface for us."

"Acting as—" He remembered Histly saying he was the best augmentation, though he still wasn't sure what she meant. He looked down at Fidi. "Anyway," he said.

"We won't hurt her. We won't wake her until we're finished examining her. We will only disable things that might harm us, nothing essential to her systems." Alien hands gripped Fidi's arms and legs, reached inside Kaslin's embrace to lift her away from him. "We will take her where you and your friend can't see what we do. In a short time we'll return her to you, and then she will awaken."

One of them soothed him, twice, and the others took Fidi and drifted away into darkness.

Histly cuffed his head. "How could you let them do that?" she yelled.

"Ow," he said. "How can I stop them?"

She lifted her hands. All her poison fingernails extended at once, turning her hands into the claws of a monster. She shook her hands at the ceiling, let out a cry of rage, turned, and strode away.

Serena dropped to sit beside Kaslin, next to the grave he had dug Fidi out of. "Avoz," she said softly. "I guess she could do worse than slap you around. Perhaps I should admire her restraint, instead of wanting to murder her every time she mistreats you. Kaslin, these new relationships...."

He meshed his fingers and squeezed his hands until his knuckles ached. "I hated her so much when I first got here," he murmured. "She has her good points, though."

"Name three."

"She's really smart. She's fun to kiss. She rescued me from starvation. She's connected and rich and beautiful. I think she cares about me."

"How can you tell?"

He sighed.

"Could you really understand them when you were talking to them? Could they understand you?"

"Unless I was hallucinating the whole thing."

"Tell me what you remember."

He sat with his feet in Fidi's grave, kicking up white powder, and repeated to his mother as much of the alien conversation as he could dredge up. Most of the aliens had disappeared into darkness, but a few hovered not far from them.

"They want you to be the bottleneck in their communications?" his mother asked.

"But it's only one direction. They understand us already."

"That's putting a lot of weight on you." She placed an arm around his shoulders. "I worry about you a lot, you know. I know you always wanted to explore. I couldn't figure out how we were going to afford a career module for that. Looks like you've found a way around the financial challenge, but is this okay?"

He closed his fists on handfuls of white powder, which puffed out between his fingers. "They said I'm their creature, Mom."

"Oh, Kaslin." She hugged him. "Not much of a life your father and I made for you, is it? Always someone else's creature. I'm sorry. I thought I had a handle on it this time, when the med tech module took and I could finally earn a good salary. I thought maybe we could be our own people for once."

"It's the nicest home we've ever had," he said.

"On the most corrupt planet I've ever heard of."

"We have to learn to work the system," he said, something his father always said, only his father never knew how to do it correctly. Kaslin and his mother cringed at his father's words coming out of his mouth, then smiled at each other.

"I guess Harvard was right about something," she said. "Law of averages: he can't always be wrong. So how are you going to work the system?"

"Histly owns my work contract, I guess, though that's something I should check when I get access to the web. She got me a job with her father's company, and an office, Mom."

"You got that for yourself," Histly said. She slid down beside him, on the side away from his mother. Her augmented fingernails were back in hiding, and she looked resigned. "He asked Dad for a partnership in the caverns exploitation enterprise, and Dad said all right."

"Partnership? Caverns exploitation?"

"Histly and her father see a lot of commercial potential here," said Kaslin. He held up a handful of white powder. "The things this can do when it's properly addressed. The potential products and merchandising from first contact. Histly appointed me ambassador, and I guess the aliens agree. I'm in a better position to work the system than I was before."

"Looks like it," said his mother.

"Can we recruit you, too?" Histly asked Serena.

"Why?"

"You got the full treatment, didn't you? Like Kaslin's?"

"I don't have the equipment to make that assessment yet. We resemble each other more than we resemble other people who have been altered by aliens—our sample being limited to us, you, and my partner Avari. I don't have the language, which I would think is the most valuable tool for dealing with them."

"That will change," said Histly. "We'll get the language, even if they don't give it to us. We have excellent linguists on staff."

"What can you offer me?" Serena said.

"We can double or triple your salary and put you on the board of the new corporation. We'll need you to work with the aliens and the other things down here. Our labs don't seem capable of analyzing what we've found yet. We may need to develop new analytical equipment." She picked up some powder, held it out. "This stuff reacts negatively to most of what we've got. It goes dead away from here and Kaslin. We've got to reverse that if we're going to use it commercially."

"Wow," said Serena.

"Told you she was smart, Mom."

She stroked his head, his shoulder, his arm. It was the same soothing motion the aliens always made, and he wondered who had taught it to whom. "You did," she said.

An alien wandered out of the dark, leading Fidi. She looked as she had at supper; she had all her hair, and even her clothes. She let go of the alien's hand and raced to Histly, dropped to hug her.

"Are you all right, piglet?" Histly asked. She hugged Fidi and released her, then studied her closely. "They promised they wouldn't hurt you."

"I feel okay," Fidi said. "I woke up in the dark, though, surrounded by giant spiders, and there weren't any humans there. I was scared."

"We've got you now. Your augs might not act right, though. The spiders might have messed with them."

Fidi stretched out her fingers. Hidden fingernails shot out, and she examined each of them before retracting them. "I don't know. All of it still looks functional." She stuck out her feet, clicked her heels together, popped blades from the front of her feet, retracted them. She did the same thing with her elbows, then altered her hands and returned them to normal. She blinked, glanced around, then looked at her sister. "It all feels the same."

"Huh," said Histly.

"You children are terrifying," Serena said.

"You could do all that and you never told me?" Kaslin asked Fidi.

"What? Why should I tell anybody? They're just for emergencies. Besides, I didn't want to get a rep like Histly's."

A group of aliens returned. They excavated a second mound.

In moments, they had laid bare a sleeping Mr. Mapworth. They lifted him. "This one will take longer," one of them said to Kaslin. "He's the one you told us about, correct?"

"Yes."

"Excellent." They floated off silently into darkness again, Mr. Mapworth carried in a hammock of alien arms, leaving two of their number to watch the rest of the graves and the small human party.

"Now, I'd like to get back to Avari," said Serena, "and maybe get aboveground again, though what we'll find when we get there—absent without reason for—" she checked her wrist—"nearly a day—" Her eyes narrowed. "I must fetch Avari. The hack on our locators isn't working anymore, and someone above is looking for me. Kas, I'm turned around from where I was last time I saw him. Can your friends tell us where he is?"

Kaslin scrambled to his feet, pulled Histly up, too. Fidi rose with them. They all approached one of the guard aliens. "Can you tell us where Avari is?" Kaslin asked.

"Not far," said the alien. It reached out, tapped on his temple. A three-dimensional map sprang up around him, showing all the turns and windings of the caverns; it stretched out farther around him than he could see. The alien moved furry fingers through it, and one of the rooms lit green. "We are here," it said, "and the other is here." It traced a green-glowing path down the big chute, along three tunnels, through a couple of small pocket caves to another cavern, which glowed orange when tapped.

Kaslin studied the route three times, tracing it in his mind.

Histly grabbed his shoulder and shook it. "What are you doing?"

"Checking a map. Stop that."

"A map?" Her voice was excited.

"I think I have it," he said, and the alien stopped pressing on his forehead. The map vanished. Kaslin raised two fingers to his forehead and pressed the same place, and the map sprang into sight again. "Wow!"

The alien soothed him and went back to guarding the mounds.

"You have a map?" Histly said.

"Apparently I do. Let's go." He stopped pressing his forehead and headed for the big chute down into the lower cavern. The others followed.

"We're going to need a map," Histly said as they sat at the top of the chute and pushed off.

"I'll see what I can do about recreating it when we get home. Bike! Bike! Bike bike bike!"

The floor rose up, wrapped them in welcoming stretchy white veils that stopped them from shooting across the cavern floor. The veils settled down around them as soon as they stopped. Kaslin brushed off his pants and rose to his feet, as did the others. He led the way in a new direction, one that had no footprints. He had to speak the floor hard as he went. Fidi ran on ahead of them and sank into the floor up to her arms. "What?" she cried, flailing and digging herself in deeper.

"You never had time to get used to this place, did you?" Histly hauled her out onto solider ground. "You have to wait until Kaslin makes it safe."

"How does he do that? Oh, the hardening word. What's the hardening word, Kas?"

"Blook."

Fidi knelt, plunged her hand in the soft flakes ahead of them. "Blook," she said. She lifted her hand and a wad of floor clung to it like a cast. "Wah!" She shook her hand, but the clump encasing it didn't drop off. "Ka-as." She made the one syllable into two.

"Damn! You can make it work, too? Unfair!" yelled Histly.

"'Buk' is the softening word," Kas said.

"Buk. Buk buk buk buk buk!" Fidi said. She shook her hands and the flakes flaked away. "Wah. Thanks. So I say my words and direct them to parts of the floor?"

"I guess." Kaslin couldn't remember directing the words anywhere, but since Fidi had observed the words working on some of the flakes and not all of them, he'd been more conscious of how strangely specific the words were. When he had first come down into the cavern, he had said a lot of words with no visible effect. What was "bootah," anyway?

Fidi rose. "Where are we going, Kas?"

He pointed to a tunnel across the cavern. "That opening."

"Oh. Okay. Blook!" she yelled, and ran toward the opening, then leaned forward and slid all the way there.

"What?" he muttered.

Fidi held out her hands. "Bike!" she yelled as she headed for the cavern wall. The floor rose up and stopped her before she hit. When she clawed out of the veils, she was laughing. "This is so stellar!"

She had made the path with one word, instead of a stream of repeated sounds. Kaslin hadn't even imagined doing that. He walked the path she had left. It was wide and strong.

"Recruit the child for practical applications design," Serena said to Histly.

"I will. After I beat her up for getting what I want without even having to ask for it."

"My data are changing, Kas," Serena said. "They're not simply choosing to make their modifications of us based on whether we're augmented or unmodified. The aliens are making quirky choices."

"We need a larger sample size," Kaslin said. "I wonder how Mr. Mapworth's going to come out."

"Why are you walking when you can slide?" Fidi called. She darted into the tunnel entrance. "Blook!"

"Wait," Kaslin yelled. "There are some branchings in there—" He ran after her, Histly at his heels, and tried sliding, which worked too well. He slid right into the tunnel, screaming, which made a satisfying amount of noise. "Bike!" he cried just before he hit the wall. The ground saved him. He wondered if "bike" overrode "blook." Probably, if Fidi had changed the whole tunnel floor to hard. Maybe subsequent words overrode all previous ones.

"Fidi!" Histly yelled when she had freed herself from the veils of floor. "Get back here!"

Fidi skated back, her laughter echoing in the tunnel.

"She is *so* irritating," Histly muttered.

So quickly adapted to the new environment, Kaslin thought. He pressed the map spot on his forehead and checked the image around him, saw that a small pink cloud hovered in the image of the tunnel where they were now, and the glow around the cavern they had started in had dimmed. "We're pink," he muttered, studying the green thread of the path ahead. "All right."

When they rounded a corner and found three branches of tunnel, they also found Fidi tasting a wall. "Buttered cornroot," she said, and stuck her tongue out, grimacing. "Where now?"

Kaslin led them down the right-hand way, musing about how useful he was going to be to the Mapworth corporation once Fidi could do everything he could do, and do it better. He had to lock in whatever benefits he could get now. He wondered if she had the map in her head. "Fidi?"

She raced back to him, still smiling, her lips edged with powder. She licked them. "Burnt bread," she said. "I never told anyone I like the taste."

"I want to try an experiment."

"Okay."

He felt his own map spot first, then reached across and tapped her forehead in a similar spot. "Tell me if you see anything."

"Like what?"

"A map of the caverns."

She glanced around as he pressed various places on her forehead, but finally said, "Nothing, and I'm getting a headache."

"Sorry."

"Kaslin," said his mother, nudging his shoulder. "Someone's tripped my locator. We have to get out of here."

"Sorry," he said again, and led them to Avari without stopping for any other explorations.

Avari was awake but entombed in the wall, except for his head, which still had most of its hair. "Serena," he cried. "Thank everything!"

"Buk buk buk," she muttered to the wall, and scratched at it with her hands. "Someone aboveground knows where we are now."

"Kas? Who are these girls?" Avari asked as Serena freed his

hands. He dug and pushed himself out of the wall as soon as it softened enough and he could get leverage.

"These are my schoolmates, Histly and Fidi Etasha."

"What are they doing down here?"

"Histly got here before you did," he said. "She chased me down here in the first place. Fidi came down with the second expedition."

"There's an expedition? How long have I been unconscious?" He checked his chrono. "Shysse," he said. "Damn it, Serena, you should have let me call. Who mounted an expedition? The gov doesn't use young girls to explore."

"We're in Mapworth country now," Serena said.

"Mapworth!" said Avari as though the name were a curse.

Histly held up a poison-nail-tipped finger, pointed it toward Avari's face. "Don't give me an excuse to use this," she said.

He held up his hand and flexed his fingers, showed that he had nails to match hers.

"Stop it," Kaslin said, "unless you both want to be trapped in a wall again."

"What?" asked Histly.

"Bike!" Fidi said. Again, she had a much firmer command of the language than Kaslin had. In one word, she accomplished what would have taken him sentences. The wall mobilized; the floor mobilized; both Histly and Avari stood in white tubes.

"Fidi," said Kaslin.

Fidi laughed. "All right, buk," she said, and the cocoons fell away from them.

Avari staggered at the sudden freedom, caught himself against the wall, snatched his hand away. "What is this?" he yelled.

"Opportunity," said Serena dryly, "knocking."

"I don't like it!"

"That's all right. Somebody else already opened the door. Come on, Avari. Let's go report."

Kaslin led the way back to the cavern entrance. As he walked, he wondered. He had special mods the others hadn't gotten: language, map. Maybe he should hoard those, try to prevent anybody else from getting them. But that might not be in the aliens' best interests. Chances were the aliens would do whatever they liked and he wouldn't be able to dictate who got which changes. Fidi had more power than the others—unless he considered Mom; he didn't know the extent of her powers.

At the first chute, they faced a nearly vertical wall of white, and there were no nearby aliens to carry them up. Kaslin glanced at Histly. "I'll take you," she said. She kicked her hands and feet into climbing tools, then bent over to offer him access. Kaslin climbed on her back, smiled at his mother, wondered what she'd make of this. He leaned into Histly's back, closed his eyes.

"Don't fall asleep," Histly murmured. "I expect you to feed me on the way up, like you did last time."

He sighed. That was going to look good. Then again, his mother had already seen him doing more with Histly than kissing food into her. No telling how long she'd been watching them in the pit.

Fidi kicked her heels and deployed her foot blades. Avari kicked his heels, too—seemed like he had the same augmentation set as the Etashas, which Kaslin found interesting. Avari must have money, or come from an important family, or both.

Serena gazed up the chute at the faraway opening at the top, studied her nearly normal hands and feet, then glanced behind her. An alien approached, picked her up, and climbed the slope ahead of them.

"I want feet that walk up walls," Histly said. She, Avari, and Fidi picked their way up the slope.

"You've got them," said Fidi.

"I want to walk like the spiders do instead of poking and picking along. This is almost like work. Hit me, baby."

Kaslin tasted the powder she offered him. Sour grapes. "I'm not sure—" he said, but she offered her mouth, so he kissed and fed her anyway. She liked it. She gave him some to store.

The others reached the top before Kaslin and Histly, since Kaslin and Histly kept stopping for samples. Histly set Kaslin down as soon as they got to the plateau, but she kept him there, kissing, as the others went on.

At the site where Fidi and Mr. Mapworth had been buried, the other five mounds had been excavated, but the people still lay in the holes in the ground, sleeping.

"Are you going to study them?" Kaslin asked the alien who stood beside his mother.

"We already have," said the alien. "These, too, are changed from their blueprints, but in different ways. Your species has gotten manipulative."

"Why shouldn't we?"

It blinked all three eyes and gave him a lipless smile.

A great group of aliens arrived. Five of them stooped to pick up the sleeping people, and another had Mr. Mapworth in some of its arms. He was dressed and seemed relaxed but possibly not conscious.

They all trooped to the base of the first chute.

"Are you coming with us?" Kaslin asked the aliens.

"Yes. It's time for our first foray back into the upper world," said one. "We need to start laying out nets. You'll speak for us?"

It wouldn't take long for the xenolinguists to take apart the alien language and make teaching modules for everybody. Kaslin straightened. Histly thought she owned him; aliens did anything they wanted to him, and called him their creature. His father sold him without asking.

It made a change from being ignored.

He wasn't sure what his new job at Mapworth entailed, but ambassador was one of his titles. Maybe he could do this in a way that helped everyone involved.

First contact, and what came after. It was something he'd wanted all his life. "Yes," he said.

One of the aliens picked Kaslin up and started up the slope with him. The others followed, including those who carried the sleeping members of the expedition. Kaslin glanced back, saw Histly looking grumpy, her arms crossed, being carried by one of the aliens. Fidi and Serena and Avari were being carried, too; Serena and Fidi were calm. Avari was limp.

The aliens set Histly, Serena, and Fidi on their feet and released them.

Histly's hand clutched Kaslin's, and he led everyone out into the upper world.